VIOLENT SATURDAY

By the Same Author
Ill Wind

VIOLENT SATURDAY

by W.L. Heath

Introduction by Edward Gorman

A Black Lizard Book

CREATIVE ARTS 1985

For
Will and Granny and Uncle Jack,
and also for my father

INTRODUCTION

By Edward Gorman

During the 1940s any number of bright young men (and women, too, when one considers Marita Wolff) got the idea of fusing John O'Hara's naturalism with the American crime novel. O'Hara himself, given parts of *Appointment in Samarra* and several of his short stories, had the same idea.

Most of this hybrid was superficially engaging but spiritually bogus. From big best-sellers such as Joseph Hayes's *The Desperate Hours* to any number of assembly-line jobs such as the novels of Vin Packer (who seemed to write either brilliantly or terribly), the hybrid became a staple voice of pop fiction. Hollywood thrived on the formula of crime-novel-meets-Balzac and gave us endless hours of the wooden stuff.

What the form awaited was an idiosyncratic voice that was as much out of Sherwood Anderson as O'Hara.

Enter W.L. Heath and *Violent Saturday*.

The year was 1955. Ike slumberingly presided over a nation spent from the McCarthy days and fixing an empty eye on the shapely new Chevvies and Marilyn Monroe's underwear. Mob entertainment, as F. Scott Fitzgerald always snottily called it, still owed more to Cecil B. De Mille than to D.W. Griffith or (God forbid) Fritz Lang. That year Georgia Gibbs had a big hit record with "Dance with Me, Henry."

Into these pieties and banalities came Heath, with the integrity of a real writer and the ear of a man who can transmute everyday conversation into poetry.

The milieu of *Violent Saturday* is the small-town South in the mid-fifties. World War II and the Korean conflict are felt here but more in the tongue-loosening effects of country club booze than in the social mores—blacks, for example, are still very much niggers and the social system is immutably good ole boy. At parties the middle-class whites put all their whiskey jokes on Jews, blacks and Catholics. Cokes get "spiked" and the funniest bits of dialogue are "a little on the rough side." Sitting at the country club (in one of Heath's beautiful phrases) "was a good expensive feeling."

Easy enough to put all this down to Southern crackery, particularly if, as they undoubtedly were, most readers were Northern, white and reasonably liberal.

But Heath is not interested in the growing black resentment that gathers storm-like on the periphery of his story; nor does he even once give us a glimpse of a Jimmy Carter-like New Southerner. Instead, he simply reports what he's heard and seen as a son of the South. If he dislikes this or that character, it's not because he or she is a bigot, or because he or she represents red-neckism in its many hues, rather only because he or she is failed in some profound moral way. Heath is not an issues man and his book is all the braver and better for it.

But what of the crime element? Is this truly a thriller or not?

The reason you hold this particular edition in your hands is because Heath took the raw pulp of dozens of other novels and shaped it into something better than its sources. Graham Greene has made a career of doing exactly this. Heath has pulled it off at least twice, giving us both thriller and novel.

The three city men whom we see in the first scene of the novel come to the town of Morgan to rob its bank, which seems, to their flawed eyes, to be a simple enough job. They are, of course, wrong, and because of their bad judgment they will affect the lives of Morgan's citizens far more than they ever imagined.

This intersection of criminals and townspeople offers Heath a perfect format for character study and he does not fail the opportunity. At least ten vivid, unforgettable lives are presented to us in the course of the book, each rendered with just the right mixture of pity and passion. Emily Fairchild, for example, manages to be repellent and alluring at the same time, winsome and doomed. Preacher, one of the robbers, is silly and sinister simultaneously, as Shelley Martin is a good man but somewhat marred by sanctimony.

Characters and events alike rush toward the climax that Heath carefully prepares us for. The novel reads as quickly as *Ethan Frome* or *The Lodger*, one of those organic examples of fiction that Raymond Chandler refered to as "a little piece of pure art," its most "pure" aspect being its voice, which is all Heath's own despite some superificial similarities to the O'Hara school of writing.

About W.L. Heath himself: born in Lake Village, Arkansas in 1924, reared in Scottsboro, Alabama, educated in public schools, Baylor Preparatory School, and the University of Virginia, William Ledbetter Heath was given the Distinguished Flying Cross and The Air Medal with Oak Leaf Cluster for his WW II flying missions over Burma and China. After graduating from college in 1949, he became copy editor of the *Chattanooga Times*, which post he resigned to turn free-lance writer in 1953.

Heath had rather more luck than most first novelists enjoy. *Violent Saturday* was published in hard covers by a prestigious firm (Harper), was brought out in paperback by the leading softcover publisher (Bantam), and became a major Cinemascope movie starring Victor Mature. In addition, Heath's short stories were selling to the slicks, "Colliers," "Esquire," and "Cosmopolitan" among others. Obviously his career was launched in a most successful way.

To date Heath has written eight novels, with a ninth in progress. Unfortunately, because *Violent Saturday* is not quite a straight novel nor not quite a thriller, it has never received its due as an important and original look at the small-town South in its most critical period of this century. No better proof of Heath's singular style can be found than in W.R. Burnett's comment on the novel—"[Heath] is thinking for himself, and very few novelists are doing that at the present time."

Today, Heath is employed by the Fieldcrest Mills in Scottsboro, Alabama. He gave up free lancing in 1959 and while the quantity of his work suffered, the quality did not. *Ill Wind*, a second major Heath novel which this series is also reprinting, proved that his material was already of the first rank, even if he cut back on the number of future books.

W.L. Heath may be enjoyed and appreciated by just about any type of reader: the casual sort looking for action and suspense, the more thoughtful kind in search of at least modest truths.

Violent Saturday is a tone poem of sorts, recalling with affecting precision the age of convertibles and sock hops, radio shows and "loose" women. It is a harsh book filled with beauty; an elegiac book rude as an insult; a hopeful statement about a hapless world. For all its tension, there is a laconic quality to the prose that lets Heath portray his people with grace and sometimes gentle insight.

Heath shares with writers such as John D. MacDonald a dual role—that of historian as well as novelist. When MacDonald was at his peak, for instance, back in the 1950s and early 1960s when he wrote many paperback originals in the third person instead of the cozier first, he chronicled the state of Florida so carefully that his fiction has added value to an historical overview of a time and place. Heath does similarly for the town of "Morgan" and for its era and epoch. Again, while the attitudes of the white townspeople are alien to the contemporary and more liberal mind, Heath sets them down as they were, not as they should be. He shows us the dress, the architecture, the concerns and the talk of the day—especially the talk, which he transcribes with unerring accuracy. Heath captures the crackling anger, bitter wit, and a melancholy sort of kindness. Writers especially have things to learn from Heath, especially how he skethces his people quickly and vividly through dialogue.

The novel has not dated except in the merest senses. Heath's story is too elemental to be anything but timeless. From the first sentence to the melancholy last, Heath shows us that the human heart is inviolate in both its joy and sorrow, that the soul is held prisoner first and foremost by itself. Not many writers before or since have been half as wise.

PART ONE

Chapter One

The three men arrived in Morgan Friday afternoon on the two-thirty train from Memphis. They were the only strangers to get off the train that day, and several people noticed them but didn't pay them much attention. They might have been salesmen or minor businessmen of some sort. The only reason they were noticed at all was because there were three of them.

One was a tall man with a round, kind face, wearing rimless glasses and a hearing aid in his left ear. He had the look of a schoolteacher about him, maybe even a Sunday-school teacher, and although he was perspiring, he didn't seem to be bothered much by the heat. He had on a plain summer worsted suit which was wrinkled from the trip, and his hat—a white Panama with a black band—was set perfectly square on his head, as if he wasn't used to wearing a hat and had let someone else put it on for him.

The other two were about the same in height, a little taller than average, and they both wore blue gabardine suits and gray hats. The similarity ended there, however, because one was slender and neat looking, and the other was heavily built and careless about how his clothes fitted him. The heavy-set one seemed to be bothered a great deal by the heat. When they walked out on the platform to look for a cab, he had a handkerchief in his hand mopping the back of his neck, and when they didn't find a cab, he set his bag down, took off his hat and wiped the sweat from around the inside of the band. He had an undershot jaw, like a shark.

The three of them stood there for several minutes on the platform, squinting against the bright July sun; and then just as the train was pulling out, Frank Dupree, who owned one of the two taxicabs in Morgan, came driving around the corner and the neat-looking one hailed him.

"Where's the hotel?" he asked through the window of the cab.

"Over there about two blocks," Frank said. "On the corner of the square."

"Only a couple of blocks, eh?"

"Let's ride, let's ride," the one with the undershot jaw said impatiently. He was suffering from the heat.

Frank took their bags and the men got in. The tall one who wore the hearing aid sat in front beside Frank and the other two rode in the back.

"Jesus H. Christ it's hot," said the heavy one in the back seat. "I never seen anything like it in my life."

"Well, it has been bad all right," Frank said. "Dry, is the trouble. We ain't had a drop of rain here since the twentieth day of June. You ought to see what it's doing to the crops."

"What do they grow around here, anyhow?" the heavy one asked.

"Cotton mostly, and some corn."

"What about corn liquor? They grow a little of that too?"

"Oh yes, they's always been a little of that around." Frank glanced up at the rear-view mirror. "Mind me asting what you gentlemen's business is here?"

"We're with the TVA," said the neat one, lighting a cigarette. "We're down here to see about some property settlements."

Frank looked up at the mirror again, then turned the corner into the north side of the square. He expected the men to make some remark about the town—either that it looked like a nice little place to live or that it looked like a mighty dull little place to live—most newcomers did express one of those opinions when they first saw the courthouse square; but these men said nothing. They looked around taking it all in, from the confederate monument to the watermelons piled up like cannon balls beside the sulphur well; but they made no comment whatever. At the second corner Frank was stopped by a red light and as they waited for it to change, a group of Negro girls wearing blue jeans and loafers crossed the street in front of the cab. The man sitting beside Frank turned and looked at him.

"Lot of smokes in this town, I guess."

Frank was surprised by his voice. It was high and soft, not the kind of voice you expected from a man his size.

"Yeah, they's quite a few colored here." Frank said. "They don't give us no trouble however. You take Detroit, Michigan, places like that, they have more trouble with them than we do. No matter what you read, either."

When the light changed, Frank drove diagonally across the intersection and drew up in front of the hotel, an old two-story brick building with a deep porch and a deep shady balcony above it with green wrought-iron balustrades. There were a dozen or more rocking chairs on the porch and on the balcony, and in one of them at the far end of the porch, an old man wearing yellow suspenders and high black shoes was asleep. He held a fly swatter in his hand.

"Well, here you are, gentlemen," Frank said. "That'll be ten cents a head."

"Pay him, Preacher," said the man with the undershot jaw. "I got no change."

"Don't worry," the neat-looking one said. "I'm going to pay the fare."

They got out and Frank lifted their bags from the trunk and set them on the sidewalk. A Negro man wearing a white jacket such as Pullman porters wear came out of the hotel, took the three bags and followed the men inside.

Frank watched them go in and shook his head. "I doubt it, mister," he said to himself. "I doubt if the TVA ever heard of you."

The three strangers registered at the hotel as Mr. Thomas, Mr. Blake and Mr. Brown; but when they were upstairs in their room they called each other by different names. The neat one was Harper, the heavy-set one was named Dill, and the tall one with the hearing aid was called simply "Preacher." They took off their coats and hats, and the one named Dill stripped down to his underwear. He was soaked with sweat. He lit a cigar and stood by the window to get some air.

"How do you like that cabbie?" he said. "We're in his cab two seconds and already he's got to know all about us. I told you,

3

Harper. Didn't I tell you? People in a place like this, they got too much nose. We're making a big mistake. We're going about the whole thing wrong."

"No we're not," Harper said. He was looking around for a place to put out his cigarette. "He wouldn't have got curious if you hadn't said that about corn liquor. You're going to have to learn to keep your mouth shut, Dill."

"Yeah," said Preacher.

"I can keep my mouth shut," Dill said. "Don't worry about my mouth."

" 'What kinda crops you grow around here?' " Preacher said mimicking Dill. "He's got to know about the crops. Naw, we ain't worried about *your* mouth, Dill."

"All right," Dill said. "What's the matter with a question like that?" He looked at Harper. "What is this guy, funny or something? Who was it asked about the jigs?"

"Take it easy," Harper said.

Preacher loosened his shoelaces and stretched out on one of the beds. Dill looked out the window again. He could see a narrow dirt street that ran close behind the hotel, and also the back yards of half a dozen houses. To his right, looking obliquely down the dirt street, he saw a used-car lot which faced the east side of the hotel. Two men were standing at the gate of the lot, and one of them held a rolled newspaper in his right hand, slowly tapping the palm of his left hand with it as he talked. Heat shivered on the polished tops of the cars, and from somewhere in the distance came the sound of hammering on metal—the sound of work going on at a filling station or a garage. Otherwise the town was quiet.

"Well, I'll say one thing," Dill said. "We sure picked the hottest hole in the forty-eight. You feel that air coming in the window?"

"Yeah," Preacher said, and winked at Harper. "I feel plenty of hot air in this room."

Dill turned to look at him again and took the cigar out of his mouth. "I'm telling you, Preach, you better let it lie. I don't have to take anything off *you*, and that's for *sure*."

Preacher laughed softly. Harper went in to use the bathroom. "Just take it easy," Harper said. "Both of you."

"No fooling, I don't get this guy." Dill said seriously. "First he begs his way into this, and then soon as we say all right he's in, he tries to take over. Now he's going to tell me when to open my mouth and when not to."

"Sometimes that's what you need for somebody to tell you," Harper said from the bathroom.

"Yeah? Well, I don't happen to see it that way. I don't happen to see it that way at all."

"All right," Harper said. "Just don't let it upset you, will you? We got other things to think about. We got a schedule to set up."

"And I'll tell you something else," Dill went on. "He gives me the creeps with that voice of his. He gives me the plain goddam creeps."

"I told you, take it easy, Dill."

Preacher was lying on his back, gazing up at the ceiling and smiling. He adjusted his hearing aid. "What do we do this afternoon, Harp?"

"We go down and take a good look. We check a few things that need checking—such as the car, for instance—and then we walk around and look some more."

"In other words," Dill said, "we get seen by as many people as we can. Is that it? I think you're out of your mind."

Harper flushed the commode and came out of the bathroom tightening his belt. "All right, look, Dill," he said. "What difference is it going to make who sees us and who don't? They don't know us, and they never will, chances are. All we got to concentrate on is getting back to Memphis. Once we make Memphis we're all right."

"You think we'll ever get to Memphis?"

"If Slick holds up his end, I know we will."

"I don't know about that Slick," Dill said. "I got no confidence in a nigger, never have."

"Slick's all right, Anyhow it's simple, what he has to do."

Dill shook his head. "Niggers scare too easy. Up in Council Bluffs we had us a nigger, remember? He gummed the works but good, that nigger did."

"Don't worry about Slick though," Harper said. "Slick's going to be all right."

"Yeah," Preacher said. "Don't worry about nothing, Dill. Just the mouth is all we want you to worry about." He closed his eyes and gave a high soft giggle.

Dill looked at Harper. "No crap, Harper, don't he give you the creeps? Listen at that laugh, will you? I swear to God."

Preacher raised himself on one elbow and looked at Dill. He looked him over from head to foot—a hairy, pot-bellied man with a big nose and no chin at all. "You know what you ought to do, Dill?" he said. "You ought to try changing your underwear once in a while."

"Go to hell," Dill said, turning back to the window. Over the tops of the trees he could see the semaphores and the peaked roof of the railway station they had just left. He sighed and tapped his cigar ashes into a corner of the window sill. "Well," he said, "this is it, eh? The mighty metropolis of Morgan, Alabama."

2

Shelley Martin, who worked as an expediter for the Fairchild Chenille Company, was one of those who saw the three men when they arrived in Morgan that day. Shelley had gone to the Express office to ship a case of rug samples, and when he came out again and walked across the platform to his car, he saw them standing there in the sun, looking for a taxi. He noticed that they were strangers, all apparently traveling together, and he wondered more or less automatically who they were and what they were doing in Morgan. But that was as far as it got with Shelley. He had other things on his mind. The train was still in the station, panting and sighing in the blistering heat when Shelley backed his car out and drove away toward the Fairchild plant. He didn't see the men get into Frank Dupree's cab; he didn't even give them a second thought.

Among other things, Shelley was thinking about going fishing. The next day was his day off, and if the weather held, as it was more than likely to do, he thought a man might catch some fish. The bass were feeding at the surface now, coming up for the willow flies along the bank at sundown. He went over it in his mind as he drove, thinking where he might go and what sort of lure would be best. Probably a white popping bug with feather streamers, he decided. A white popping bug was a hard lure to beat.

When he stopped in front of the long two-story brick-and-glass building that was the Fairchild main plant, he picked up a clipboard from the seat beside him and walked across the pavement toward a door marked "Office." But before he reached the door it was opened by a well-dressed middle-aged man who paused to light a cigarette and then started down the flagstone walk toward the private parking area. When the man saw Shelley he stopped again and came back a few steps to meet him.

"What did you find out on the Ward order, Shelley?"

"Well, nothing yet," Shelley said, "except that nineteen sets of 22-23's have disappared in mid-air. I've just come from the station. Had to mail some samples for Daisy."

"Well, if the stuff doesn't show up, just ship the rest of the order and wire them a new date on the shortage. It'll have to be made, I guess. You can check with Boyd on it."

"That's where I'm headed now, to see Boyd."

Mr. Fairchild glanced at his watch, then up at the sky and smiled. "Fish ought to bite on a day like this, Shelley."

"I was thinking the same thing myself. I may try them tomorrow—want to go along?"

"No, I wish I could, but I've got to go to Birmingham." He looked at his watch again. "Matter of fact, I'm going to have to step on it, too, if I make that train."

"Well, have a good trip."

"Thanks. See you Monday."

Shelley pushed through the glass door into the office and immediately felt a release from the heat. Three girls were typing at desks along the left side of the room, and on the right a man wearing horn-rimmed glasses was talking into a phone. All three of the girls looked up as Shelley came in, and one of them, a bosomy blonde in a green batiste blouse, raised her hand and wriggled her fingers at him. He walked across the room to the water cooler, had a drink and then opened the door to the inner office. The floor was carpeted in Mr. Fairchild's private office, and there were leather chairs and ashtrays and big pictures of the Muscle Shoals dam along the back wall.

Behind one of the two mahogany desks sat a good-looking young man wearing a seersucker suit and a blue Oxford cloth shirt with a button-down collar. He was Boyd Fairchild. On the green blotter in front of him there was an expensive camera and several small round pieces of colored glass.

"What's that?" Shelley said, pointing to the camera.

"That's what they call a Leica," Boyd said. "It was made in Germany and I paid three hundred dollars for it. Everybody says I'm nuts; what do you say?

"I say you're nuts too."

Boyd laughed and pushed the camera away. "What's on your mind, Shelley?"

"This Ward order." Shelley settled himself in one of the leather chairs. "Are you right sure it was all stamped, Boyd?"

"Sure I'm sure." He opened his desk, thumbed through a large loose-leaf book and pulled out a page. "See here? Four hundred 22-23's—two hundred blue, a hundred chartreuse and a hundred yellow. That's the whole order, rugs and lids, made up July the first."

Shelley pushed his hat back and shook his head. "We haven't got it though. So help me, we've looked every-damn-where and there's only eighty-one of the yellow."

"Well—"

"Wait a minute," Shelley said. He picked up the phone and dialed a number. "I just had an idea. Hello, Clyde? This is Shelley. Listen, how about checking back there with Buck and see if he's got any overs in style 22-23, will you?"

"What color, Shelley?"

"Any color. I want to know all your overs in that style."

There was a long silence, and as they waited, Shelley took a pack of cigarettes from his pocket, shook one out and reached for the big silver lighter on Boyd's desk.

"Shelley?"

"Yeah?"

"We got nineteen sets of pink with no order against them."

"That's what I thought," Shelley said. "Thanks." He hung up and looked at Boyd. "There's your missing yellow. The stuff was dyed the wrong color."

"*Dyed* wrong? How could that happen?"

"Somebody put the wrong number on the dye ticket, I guess.

They wrote down a seven when it ought to have been a six."

"I still don't see it," Boyd said. "Eighty-one of them came out the right color. Why would nineteen get put off in another tub under a different number?"

"Well, the dye runs are made up by weight," Shelley said. "If eighty-one happened to fill out say a two-hundred-pound run of yellow, the other nineteen had to go in another run. Trouble is, they got put in the wrong tub."

"Oh," Boyd said. "Well, I guess they'll have to be made over. I'll write a new stamping order." He picked up a pad, then looked at Shelley again. "Who do you suppose made a mistake like that?"

"I don't know, but I can find out. It's bound to happened in the laundry."

"What do you think I ought to do?"

"Nothing. Let him know you don't like it, and then if it happens again, fire the hell out of him."

Boyd laughed. "You'd be rough on him, would you, Shelley?"

"If it happened again I would."

"I believe you would too."

They both laughed, and Shelley got up to go. The door opened suddenly and the girl in the green blouse looked in. "Your wife just called, Boyd," she said. "She said tell you she was going to play golf."

"Did she say who she was going with?"

"No, she didn't"

There was a fraction of silence and Shelley was careful not to look up. He thought Boyd was probably sorry he'd asked that.

"Okay, thanks, Jane."

The girl closed the door and Boyd got up and walked around in front of his desk. "Shelley, I've got the fishing fever."

"So has everybody else."

"You think they'd hit, or is too hot?"

"They'll hit. I'm planning to try them myself tomorrow. I asked your dad and he turned me down; what about you?"

"Yeah, I would, Shelley. What time will you leave?"

"Oh, I don't know. Four would be early enough, I guess. The bass won't feed till nearly dark, but we could fish for bream awhile first."

"All right, count me in. Can you come by for me?"

"All right. Around four okay?"

"Fine. And I'll bring along a bottle of lunch."

As Shelley drove back down Lemon Street toward the warehouse and shipping department, he thought about Boyd and wondered a little about the future of the Fairchild Chenille Company. That boy ought to be doing better than that, he thought. He ought to at least know how a dye run is made up, long as he's been in that office. He don't seem to have his mind on business. Well, too much wife, maybe. She's carrying him too fast. Too much wife and too much money. It can ruin you. It can sure as the world mess you up.

3

The three strangers walked slowly around the courthouse square, two in front and the tall one walking behind. They passed the barber shop and the hardware store and went around the south side past the fire hall, the Masonic building and the telegraph office. When they came to the drugstore, the neat-looking one went in, leaving the other two waiting out front. He bought a pack of gum and some cigarettes and asked Dr. Huff, the pharmacist, if there was a U-drive-it in town.

"No, there isn't," Dr. Huff told him. "We've got a couple of taxicabs, but no U-drive-it."

"No place where a man might rent him a car?"

"I'm afraid not," Dr. Huff said.

Harper thanked him and went out again to where Dill and Preacher were waiting.

"What did you find out?" Dill said, mopping his neck with his handkerchief.

"No luck. We'll have to do a little figuring."

"I don't like the sound of that," Dill said.

"Don't worry, I'll come up with something."

They walked on in the bright, hot sun, and the one named Dill looked tired and miserably hot. Preacher, walking behind, was jingling the change in his pocket and whistling softly. They passed the movie theater and a restaurant and then a big glass door that listed the names of several dentists and lawyers who had their offices upstairs. Not many people were on the streets. After a while, when they had made a complete circuit of the square, they crossed the street to the courthouse lawn and sat down on an iron bench under one of the shady maple trees. Several pigeons were waddling around near the big green Civil War cannon.

"Now what?" Preacher said.

"I'm going over to the bank before it closes," Harper said. "You two can wait here or either go on back to the room."

"I'm going to wait right here in the shade," Dill said. "This is the coolest place I've found."

"I may walk around some more," Preacher said. "I like this little burg. I seen a movie once about a little town like this with Mickey Rooney in it."

They were silent for a while, and then Dill said: "Movies. They're hell nowdays, ain't they? Whatever happened to the good movies they used to have?"

"I don't think they're so bad," Preacher said. He adjusted the wire of his hearing aid. "What do you want for fifty cents?"

"I want something besides a horse opera. That's all they make any more, stupid cowboy pictures. In gorgeous Technicolor. Three out of ever four you see any more is a horse opera. I like a good comedy myself. What ever happened to Laurel and Hardy and that bunch?"

"The one I like is that June Allyson."

"You would," Dill said. "She's so cute I could puke."

"All right, who *do* you like?"

"I like Bogart okay. And that number that played in the one where the guy gets the chair in the end—what was the name of that?"

"You mean where he knocks this broad up and then has to drown her in the lake?"

"That's it. What was the name of that?"

"*A Place in the Sun.*"

"*A Place in the Sun* is right. That number in that show was strictly all right, you know that? Elizabeth Taylor her name was."

Harper thumped his cigarette away and got up. "Well, I'm

11

going on. You boys do whatever you like and we'll meet back at the hotel in say an hour."

"I'm staying put," Dill said. "I like the feel of this shade, myself."

4

Emily Fairchild didn't really like to play golf; she wasn't good at it, and it bored her; but she did like the idea of golf. It was smart to play. Golf dresses were nice, too, and she looked good in them, and there was something pleasant about being out there in the sun on one of the big smooth greens with a Negro caddie holding the pin and the little red flag fluttering in the breeze. It made a nice scene. And then after you had played a round, it was even nicer to sit on the long cool upstairs porch of the clubhouse and look down through the pines at the other golfers. That was the best part of it, really, Emily thought. When the game was over and you were sitting up here on the porch, sipping a Coke and talking. It was a good expensive feeling.

"What time is it, Madge?" she said. "I left my watch."

"Nearly four-thirty," Madge said. "Steve and Boyd should be out soon."

"I don't know if Boyd's coming or not," Emily said.

They were sitting on a long, varnished pine bench near the top of the stairs, and Emily, who had taken off her shoes, sat with her feet up on the porch rail, relaxing.

"You better get your feet down," Madge said.

"What for?"

"Well, if somebody happened to walk out down there on the terrace they'd get a good look at your fanny, that's what for."

"They wouldn't see anything they haven't seen before." Emily said. But she took her feet down anyway and crossed her legs. "Who's that? Down there on the eighth tee."

"Looks like Ed and Bobby Parks, from here."

"No, I mean the other one, in the checkered shirt."

"Oh, that's Harry Reeves. You know. At the bank."

"Is that Harry *Reeves*?"

"That's him. Can't you see those buck teeth? I can see them from here."

"Well, I never," Emily said. "Lord, that checkered shirt. It makes him look about two hundred years younger."

"From a distance anyway."

"When on earth did he join the club?"

"Search me. Probably since that new nurse moved to town. She plays occasionally, and you know what they say about Harry, don't you?"

"I've heard some gossip," Emily said, "but I don't necessarily believe it. Not Harry Reeves. Not with five children."

"That's what they say, though. They say he follows her down the street with his tongue practically hanging out of his mouth."

"Who's they?"

"Several I've heard."

"What about the girl? Is she supposed to be leading him on or something?"

"I guess so. I don't know. To tell you the truth, I get most of my information through Janis Beckly, and you know Janis. There may not be a word of truth in it."

"May not be is right," Emily said. "Honestly. She's a fine one to talk, isn't she? After the way she carried on for years around here with that—*character*."

"You mean the one that was here with the TVA? Zimmerman, I think his name was."

"Anyway he was a Jew."

Madge finished her Coke, belched and set the empty bottle on the floor beside her. "Going back to Reeves," she said, "I also heard another version of it. I heard he doesn't even know the girl. Just follows her around and things like that."

"Well, that's worse," Emily said. "That's pitiful."

"I'll tell you something else, too. He's not the only man in town who's given her a second look. Do you know her?"

"I've seen her is all. She came out here to a party one night with Bill Clayton, but I didn't meet her. Luckily."

"She's not bad looking, I'll say that for her."

"Oh now really, Madge. She looks like a goddam chorus girl, if you'll pardon my French."

"The thing is, most men happen to like chorus girls," Madge said. She got up and stretched. "I've got to run down and water the cat. Be back in a minute."

"Leave me a cigarette," Emily said. "I forgot mine."

"You forget everything. They're on the rail there in front of you. By the way, did I tell you about mother losing her purse."

"No. How much was in it?"

"Fifty dollars."

"Wow. Did she lose it in town or where?"

"In town she thinks. She's running an ad in the Lost and Found, but I told her she'll never see that money again."

"Probably not," Emily said. "That's too bad."

"You bet it's too bad. Fifty dollars is fifty dollars. Well, I'll be back in a minute."

Emily watched her go down the stairs, then she lit a cigarette and relaxed, looking down the slope through the big pines.

Presently she heard the sound of golf shoes grating on the stone terrace. She leaned over the rail and saw Pete Brayley and his wife and Dink Hartman coming up from the locker rooms. Dink, who was something of a joker in their crowd, had a towel in his hip pocket that hung almost to his heels. All three of them had Coke bottles in their hands, and Dink looked as though his might have something a little stronger than Coke in it.

"Hi," Emily called.

Dink looked up, whipped off his cap and bowed deeply. He was drinking all right; Dink was always drinking on Friday afternoons. "Well," he said. "If it's not Miss Emily Unfairchild. Come on down and have a toddy."

"What is it?"

"I don't know. Calox, Hadacol or something. Come on down."

The Brayleys laughed; they had been drinking too, Emily noticed.

She decided to go down.

Chapter Two

It was six-thirty when the three men came down from their room in the Commerce Hotel and went out for supper. Sugarfoot, sitting in his little rattan chair by the door, saw them go and checked their departure by the clock. Sugarfoot was the

14

bellhop at the Commerce. He was the one who carried their bags in and put up the third bed in the double room, and he had taken an uncommon interest in them from the first.

What they up to? he wondered, watching them pause there at the foot of the steps, and then, without saying a word to each other, walk slowly away, two in front and the tall one walking behind.

What they doing in a town like this you suppose?

Sugar had studied about it all afternoon and still he couldn't pigeonhole those three. It worried him. There were lots of pigeonholes in old Sugar's head, and it was a rare traveler who didn't fit into one of them. But these three had him stumped. The fact that they were together was what had him really stumped. Take them one at a time and I might could handle them, he thought. Take that least one, he's going to be a gambler, most likely; that cigar might of come here to book in a stage show at the Ritz; and old tall-boy with that thing in his ear, he look to me like some kinda preacher, down here to hold a protracted meeting and pick up some change. But man, you cain't put all that together in one room. Naw, Sugar, he told himself, you ain't seen nothing of that style before.

He looked around the lobby and sighed. I got to have me another little smell of that bottle before long, he thought. It don't look like that last one going to see me through. I got to wait awhile though. I got to stretch it some tonight; ain't but half a pint between me and midnight. I got to rubber-band that stuff tonight.

Sugarfoot drank steadily and heavily, but there was no one in Morgan who had ever seen him staggering drunk. He knew how to gauge it, was why. He knew how to get himself up there just right and stay that way for days, even weeks, if the money held out. He never bruised it, never tried to mess around. "You cain't mistreat it, man," he told them. "First thing you know you done met yoself face to face in the bottom of a toilet bowl. Sick? Man alive! Or worsen that, some dark night something liable to come up behind you softly." He didn't bruise it any; didn't try to crowd it at all. And at six-thirty he knew he had till eight, at least, before he made another trip behind the stairs to his bottle.

The lobby was quiet, and with the exception of Mr. Neff and

Sugar himself, it was deserted too. The only sounds came from the dining room where five or six traveling men and two or three permanent guests were having supper—a tinkle of silverware and a muted undertow of conversation. The drummers didn't talk much at the table. They ate. They'd do their talking afterward when they were sitting out on the porch with their cigars glowing in the dark. Mr. Kober and Mr. Tom Matthews were both in tonight, and if they could scare up a couple more there'd probably be a bridge game in the rear of the lobby till way late. Otherwise it was going to be a quiet night. No girls tonight, Sugar thought. There wasn't a sporting man in the house. Friday was always a dull night anyway at the hotel.

Sugar moved his chair around a little so he could see through the arched doorway into the dining room where the people were eating at a single long table. He noticed that Miss Benson, the nurse, wasn't eating in tonight either. That meant she had a date probably. Some of these sporting gentlemen ought to look into that, Sugar thought. Naw, that won't do, he told himself. She ain't going to mess around with no drummer. She got other fish to fry. Now there's another funny thing about them three in 201. Why don't they take supper in? We got the best food in town, ain't we? Must be that big table scared them off. Too many at one table. They ain't doing no talking, ain't answering no questions, them three. I cain't place them. I cain't put my finger on them three to save me.

He shook his head and looked out again toward the street and the soft summer dusk. Got to smell that bottle before long sure enough, he told himself. This here's Friday and Miz Neff liable to take a gret notion to play the piano. Then I *know* I got to have me one. I cain't suffer that racket. She get them fingernails to clicking on the keys and Sweet Jesus if I ever heard a instrument so abused. Rock a Ages. Lord, don't I hope she ain't got a notion to sing awhile too. I be out of a bottle before nine o'clock.

2

Shelley had stopped to get a haircut on his way home from work, and while he was in the chair a man named Ted Proctor came in for a shine and they got to talking. Ted was trying to decide what to do with his vacation which came up at the end of the month.

"I thought about Florida," he said, "but it's been so hot lately I can't see going to Florida. Louise favors a trip to the Smokies."

"It's nice over there," Shelley said. "Helen and I were over last spring. You know something? They've got wild bears over there. We saw them from the car."

"Me, I'd take Florida," the barber said. "I go for those bathing beauties." He began to laugh suddenly, remembering something, and came around in front of the chair to tell it. "We stopped at this place they call Silver Springs one time—you probably heard of it—where they have all these different kinds of fish and all? Well, we was taking a tour around the place and the guide we had happened to be a colored fellow, and he had one of these pelicans that followed him around. Pete, he called him. Pete the pelican. Well anyhow, we was looking at a bunch of alligators they had in a tub-of-a-thing there, and there was a girl in the crowd that had on a pair of shorts. This colored fellow was telling all about how dangerous these alligators are, and all at once while he's talking, this Pete the pelican waddles up to the woman in shorts and lays his beak right along the side of her bare leg. Well, I'm telling you that woman let out a screech you could of heard to Miami and jumped about three foot off the ground, and when she done that, them shorts split right up the back clear to her waist!"

They all had a good laugh, and the barber went back to work. "It beat the devil," he said, "no fooling. I like to died laughing. I swear I couldn't *help* laughing, and she was embarrassed to death, naturally. She and I guess it was her husband lit out for the car running, and every step of the way he was trying to hold his hat over her ass—I swear to God, I never laughed so hard at anything in my life."

They all laughed again and Shelley said, "Well, you can see how she must have felt, all right. And her husband too."

"I could beat that one though," Ted Proctor said. "About a woman right here in town, but it won't do to tell it."

"I think I know who you mean," the barber said. "A certain lady that got caught up near the cemetery, wasn't it?"

"That's the party. But I'd rather not repeat it."

17

"The funniest thing that ever happened around here was old Loy Baxter," Shelley said. "The time he got the pool ball hung in his mouth."

"That was good," the barber admitted. "I guess if it wasn't for Tom Huff that ball would still be in Loy's mouth. They would of buried him with a goddam pool ball in his mouth."

"What was the idea behind that anyway?" Ted asked.

"It was a bet. I think it was Handy James, or maybe Kelley himself, bet him a dollar he couldn't get a pool ball in his mouth. I was there and saw the whole thing. They had to dislocate his jaw."

"Remember Pewter Harris?" Ted said. "When he fell out of the second-floor window of the courthouse?"

"Now, that *was* something," the barber said, coming around in front of the chair again. "I happened to see that too, and so help me God, he never even let go of his broom. That's a fact. He just got up and dusted hisself off and went back up the stairs to finish his sweeping."

"What was he, an idiot or something?"

"An imbecile. Just a step ahead of an idiot. It runs in that family, you know."

"Yes, so I've heard. Wasn't he the one the train ran over?"

"No, that was old Shep Hankins' boy the train hit. He was drunk, they always thought. I don't know what ever happened to Pewter. Seems to me his sister took him up in Knoxville, finally. They had people all over Tennessee."

"Dearborn went away too, didn't he?"

"Yes, he left too."

They were silent for a while as the barber cut Shelley's hair.

"We've got some characters around here all right," the barber said. "Back in the old days seems like something was always happening. Now the town's twice as big and nothing ever happens. Looks like it would be the other way around."

3

In the meantime a party had begun to develop out at the golf club. When Emily went down to join Dink and the Brayleys, Madge came out and said she believed she'd have a small one too, and as they were going back up to the porch with their spiked Cokes, some other people showed up with another bottle. At six o'clock there were nine people up there, all drinking and talking and getting in the mood for some fun. "The best parties are always those that you don't plan," Nell Harriman remarked, and everybody agreed with her. "When a party just sort of *happens*," she said, pursuing it a little further, "that's always when it's more fun." Before long both Dink's bottle and Joey Brunis' bottle were empty, and Pete Brayley made a quick trip to town for more. It was going to be a party, all right. Everyone there was still in golf clothes except Bill Clayton, and by six-thirty things had gotten far enough along for them to insist that he go down and get into *his* golf clothes too. "Don't be antisocial," they told him. So Bill went down to the locker room and changed, and while he was down there he slipped in an extra one on them, straight. Morgan was a dry county and the bottles were always kept out of sight in the men's locker room. Liquor was never served openly except at private parties, but no one objected to drinking at the club, as long as the bottle was kept out of sight—no one, that is, except the grounds keeper's wife, and they didn't worry too much about her.

"What I should have done is brought back some weenies," Pete Brayley said. "We could have made a supper of it out here."

"I say let's sing," Dink Hartman said. "What does everyone want to sing?"

"How about 'I Been Working on the Railroad'?"

"All right, you want to start it, Nell?"

"Let Pete start it. I can't sing."

"Pete?"

"Naw, let's tell some jokes first. We're not drunk enough to sing yet."

"All right, who knows a good dirty joke?"

"I know one," Ed Parks said, "but it's a little on the rough side. I don't know if I ought to tell it yet."

"Aw, go ahead. Anybody that don't like it can leave."

"All right, here goes. It's the one about the two nuns on the train. Stop me if you already heard it."

Things went on like that for a while with Ed and Dink

19

swapping stories, and finally Pete broke down and started the singing. Martha Byjohn turned over her drink, and Joey Brunis burned a hole in Steve Whittaker's sleeve with his cigarette.

When one of the girls went down to the ladies' room, Bill Clayton moved over to sit beside Emily.

"Where's Boyd?" he said.

"I don't know. I don't think he's coming out."

"You two not spatting, I hope?"

"No. He may come out. I didn't mean to stay this late and I forgot to call him back."

"I'm glad you did," he said.

"Glad I did what, stayed late or forgot to call back?"

"Both."

She looked at him. "I said he *may* come out yet."

"All right."

"Dink, tell the one about the suppository," someone said. "You know, the dialect one."

"Aw, that's too old. You all heard that one a thousand times."

"Just the same, let's hear it."

Dink told the one about the suppository and everybody laughed.

"I still say we ought to eat," Pete Brayley said. "Why don't some good Samaritan get in his car and go to town for some weenies and potato chips and stuff?"

"Yeah, and some more liquor."

"I don't know if Steve and I'll be able to stay," Madge Whittaker said. "We've got kids at home to feed and get to bed."

"Well, what all do we need?" Bill Clayton said. "I'll go get it if one of the girls will go along with me to pick it out."

A tiny silence fell over the crowd, and a couple of the girls glanced slyly at Emily. Emily looked right back at them.

"I'll go," she said.

It was getting late now, the sun was gone and a pleasant coolness had fallen over the rolling, clipped expanse of the golf course. As they walked out through the pines to Bill's car, Emily felt suddenly annoyed with herself for what she was doing. It was an act of defiance, really; a pointless, heedless thing to have done. I wish I'd kept my mouth shut, she thought

20

to herself. I'm a fool. Now I've given them something new to say behind my back.

I'm beginning to feel my drinks a little," Bill said. "How about you?"

"A little."

"That Dink—he's a bird, isn't he?"

"He bores me. They all bore me."

"Oh-oh, somebody's in a bad humor. I wonder why."

"I don't know why. I've got a queer feeling. I think I'd like to get quietly plastered."

"Fine."

"Not with you though. Don't get excited."

He tried to take her arm as she got into the car, but she pulled away and said, "Keep cool, Casanova. We're going straight to town and straight back, so don't get any big-league ideas."

The car top was down and as they went out the curving narrow road between the trees the evening air washed against her cheeks and tossed her hair. I wonder where Boyd is, she thought. Damn it all, I shouldn't be doing this. What's the matter with me? What makes me do these fool things? She turned and looked at Bill Clayton and felt more annoyed than ever.

"Why don't you give up?" she said impulsively.

"Give what up?"

"You know damn well *what* up. Why don't you give up and get married. Get a wife of your own and stop trying to love up everybody else's. I'm getting sick of it."

He laughed, uneasily, and shook his head. "You're quite a gal, Emily, you know that?"

"Let's see, first it was Nell, then Eileen Eubanks and—"

"No, first it was you, Emily. First last and always."

"Well, it's been me for a long time, I know that. You're really persistent, aren't you? Why don't you just give it up? Get a wife of your own for a change."

Bill put his head back and laughed, not knowing exactly what else to do. He'd seen Emily like this before and it always made him uneasy. She could be entirely too plain-spoken at times, Emily could.

"All right, laugh," she said. "Give me a cigarette."

He took a silver cigarette case from his pocket, held it open for her to take one, and then depressed the dashboard lighter.

"You know what's the matter with you, Bill? You're conceited. You've got a big car and a lot of money and just because the little waitresses think you're hot stuff, you've got the same idea yourself. Well, you're not. And slow down before you kill us both."

"I'm slowing down."

"Slow down some more, then."

He looked at her and smiled, trying to get her to smile back. "You know what I think's the matter? I think you're just sorry you took me up on this in front of the other girls. You're afraid of the talk."

"Maybe so."

"You see? And what happens?—you take it all out on poor old Bill, when all I'm trying to be is nice."

"I know the kind of nice you can be, Billy Boy. Don't hand me that crap."

It was seven o'clock when they got back to the club and unloaded the hotdogs, potato chips, buns and other groceries. There was a lot of loud talk and noise coming from the dark upstairs porch now, and someone had started the phonograph in the parlor. Emily felt let-down and sober, and instead of going up the stairs with Bill, she made an excuse and walked out on the terrace. A man was standing there alone, taking deep breaths of the night air. It was Bobby Parks, and he looked as though he was about to be sick.

"Hi," he said, smiling feebly. "I had to come out for some air. Getting to be quite a party in there."

"Yeah, a sort of spontaneous demonstration."

"How did it start?"

"I don't know. It was an accident. You have anything to drink out here?"

He pointed to a Coke bottle on the edge of the terrace. "You can have that," he said, "if you don't mind drinking after me."

"I don't mind anything," Emily said. She picked up the bottle, sipped it, and then drained it. Bobby looked a little dismayed.

"Thank you, Bobby," she said. "Now tell me if I look drunk."

22

"No."

"You're a liar. I bet I look drunk as a monkey's uncle."

She smiled at him and puckered up her nose. "Thanks," she said.

She walked slowly back toward the wide steps leading to the porch and heard a woman shriek with laughter somewhere in the darkness above. She didn't want to go up there again; the party spirit had left her as suddenly as it had come on, and now she felt disgusted with herself for the things she had said to Bill. I ought to go home, she thought. I ought to at least go home and change clothes and get Boyd.

She hesitated there at the foot of the stairs, and then she saw Boyd coming toward her out of the dark, walking along the narrow path from the parking area. He had a long paper sack in his hand, which meant a bottle.

"Hello, bottle," she said.

Boyd grinned. "Why didn't you call? I was wondering what happened."

"Party."

"So I see. You look fairly sober though. What are you doing out here by yourself?"

"Waiting."

"For what?"

"Darned if I know, Boyd. Come on in and dance with me darling."

4

All around the little town the street lamps had come on now, and people were walking home or sitting down to supper or getting ready to go out to the movies. It was still hot, but at least it was night and the air was breathable again; and since this was the week-end eve there was a mild but general lifting of spirits. At the drugstore a group of high-school boys were kidding around with a boothful of girls, and on the courthouse lawn some old men had started a checker game, sitting at the edge of the monument within the yellow oblong of light that fell from the band rostrum. Working men were taking showers, baby sitters were being phoned, canasta games were being planned.

At the poolroom a round of snooker was shaping up. There were 4,700 people in the town of Morgan, and for almost every one of them Friday night meant a small but pleasant departure from the routine of weekday life. For some of them it meant choir practice at the Methodist church; for some it meant friends dropping in to watch TV; for some it meant nothing more than a quiet evening and a chance to read. But for Sugarfoot it meant just one more night like all the rest—if anything a little duller and more tedious than the others. At eight o'clock he decided on another little pop.

He got up, walked slowly around the lobby and emptied all the ashtrays into a brass pail. This was camouflage; it was something you had to do though, because if you just got up and went straight to the closet behind the stairs, you wasn't fooling anybody. Mr. Neff knew where his bottle was, of course, and when you got right down to facts, you wasn't really fooling anybody nohow. But there was such a thing as style, and also such a thing as taking care of the other fellow. Mister Neff didn't *care*, for that matter, but Miz Neff did, and you had to leave a man a way out. You had to beat around the bush a little so he could say, "I didn't notice he was drinking, Eloise. I saw him empty the ashtrays, but I didn't know he had a bottle back there." Sugar took care of Mr. Neff and Mr. Neff took care of him. Between the two of them they could pull off a lot of stuff that one man couldn't have got away with. Such as the girls, for instance. Miz Neff would be purely mortified if she knew about the girls. Mister Neff was all right. He even took a drink hisself, once in a great while when Miz went off to Nashville to visit with her sister. One time years ago, Mister Neff had got hisself so loaded up till he leaked in the potted fern, right there in the lobby. But that was just once in twenty-odd years, and it was late at night besides; no one knew it but Sugar—not even Mister Neff hisself. He could still laugh though, remembering it. Some Mister Neff all right. Miz Neff like to died when that plant turned yellow and shriveled up the way it done. She never guessed it though; never had no sign of a suspicion what happen to that plant.

Sugarfoot went down the shadowy hall and opened the closet door. He pulled the light cord and emptied the brass pail into the trash can; then he reached back in the linen shelf and brought out a pint bottle of white corn liquor. He held it up to the light and checked the level, then pulled the cork and had him a nice long one. He had a feeling in his bones that the Miz was going to play the piano tonight, and a man had to be well fuzzed-up to suffer that racket. As he tamped the cork back in place he felt the liquor spread tendrils of heat through his chest and stomach. Mighty fine, he told himself. Don't bruise it though, just shake hands with it lightly. He replaced the bottle and put out the light. When he walked back up the hall toward the lobby, he felt a familiar, secret excitement as the liquor took hold. He shifted his shoulders under the starched white jacket; he flexed his fingers and wriggled his toes in his shoes. He was right now, just about right, and the last one ought to hold till around ten o'clock.

When he took his seat again beside the open door to the porch, his mind went back to the three men in room 201. What you suppose they doing in a town like this? he asked himself again. Doggone me if I can put a finger on it. Directly I'll get to mojoing around upstairs and take another look in they room. I ought not to do that, but I got to find out something. I'm right uneasy about them three, I declare.

Supper was over and the drummers were moving out on the porch to smoke their cigars. It didn't look like a card game after all. Miss Sally Ruth Hough said she was going to the show, and Miz Neff said she believed she'd go along too, and that was a break for Sugar because it would be too late to play the piano when she got back. Things had taken a turn for the better. After it settled down again, Sugar decided to go upstairs and look around. The three men might come straight on back from supper, and if they did, he wouldn't get another chance at their room. He got up again and walked through the dining room toward the kitchen, as if he was going in to eat his supper; but at the end of the dining room he turned to his right and went through a door that opened onto the rear of the lobby where the stairs went up. Mr. Neff couldn't see him from there, and by walking softly he made it to the first landing without attracting any notice at all. The second door he passed was Miss Benson's room and as he walked by, he took her up again in his mind. I wonder if she out with Mister Ace, he thought. Mister Ace was Ace Kelley, poolroom owner and Morgan's "quality" bootlegger; Sugar had been the first to know about Miss Benson's liaison with Ace. He had taken a ten-dollar tip to lead Mister Ace up the back stairs one rainy May afternoon to Miss Benson's room. Some Mister Ace, Sugar thought. She ain't hardly two days in town till Mister Ace done got hold of the inside track. No wonder. That man always got a big pocket of change. And cain't he dress though! Man, man he got clothes for a while! But you know one thing? He cain't touch Mister Boyd Fairchild when it comes to clothes. Mister Boyd the one can dress, all right. That man stay togged out *all* the time. He got to, I guess, that wife of his. She ain't careful, she going to mess up proper, from what I hear. Don't they live high though? Some of these whites sure can live it up. Mercy. He shook his head, walking on down the hall softly.

At the door marked 201 he stopped and took a large ring of keys from his pocket. Go right on in, Sugar, he told himself. You ain't got long to mess around up here. He unlocked the door and switched on the ceiling light. What he saw told him nothing. Two of the beds were rumpled, there was an ashtray overflowing on the dresser, and in the chair beside the door was a Memphis newspaper. It might have been anybody's room, anybody at all. Sugar deliberated a moment; then, seeing the suitcases together in one corner, he crossed the room quickly and unlatched the largest of the three. When he opened it his eyes bulged. Among a few pieces of soiled clothing and towels there was a twelve-gauge shotgun with a sawed-off barrel. The gun had been taken down to fit into the bag, and the barrel was wrapped in oily brown paper.

"Gret God Amighty," Sugar said under his breath. "The Lord help us, what is I done run across now?"

Chapter Three

Elsie Cotter was a pale, persecuted woman of fifty, who looked as if the flesh of the upper half of her body had somehow loosened from the bones and settled below her waist—like a rag doll that has been shaken and pounded until

26

all the stuffing is packed into the lower extremities. Her shoulders and chest were frail, and her legs were elephantine. Miss Elsie waddled when she walked, and on this particular July evening as she was on her way home from the library, she winced a little with each waddling step, as if her ankles were hurting, or as if she had a bad headache that the delicate jarring of her footfalls made worse. She was going slowly along a shadowy street called Baird Drive, and she was thinking of the fifty dollars she'd found in a coin purse two days before, at the doorway of Rayburn's grocery store.

You couldn't possibly call it stealing (she was saying to herself) because I don't know whose it is. I honestly don't. There's no way on earth for me to return it. Just that little brass key and the two three-cent stamps, and the money; not the sign of an identification card or even a letter with an address on it. It could be almost anybody's. How, I ask you, is a person going to return money like that? You can't do it. Much as I'd like to see it back in the hands of the rightful owner, you just can't do it. Run an ad in the paper and about a dozen people would probably try and claim it.

She passed a street lamp and a bat dived out of the gloom, flitting and faltering on its soft, clothlike wings. In a house across the street a radio blared out and was quickly turned down.

Now, of course, if somebody came to me and said, "Miss Elsie, I lost a purse with fifty dollars in it in front of Rayburn's," why I'd naturally be glad to turn it over. It isn't that. It's not that I'm just trying to *keep* the money, like stealing or something like that. But after all, finders keepers, losers weepers these days. If I hadn't found it, someone else would, and no telling *who* else either. You can bet your life whoever it was would have spent it by now and not waited, the way I have, to see if it's claimed. No siree. In a way, whoever lost it is lucky it was me that found it, because nine out of ten would have just said well good for me and spent it on themselves without giving it so much as a second thought by now. I'll be more than glad to turn it over to the rightful owner, the minute they identify themself. That's a trait the Morgan family has *always* had.

She turned right at the Methodist church and waddled painfully along Merton Street, where the houses were smaller and set closer together. She could hear dishes clattering in kitchens as the housewives cleaned up after supper. Somewhere a screen door slammed, and then, distantly, a dog barked.

Of course I'm not going to hold onto that money for*ever*, she thought. After all, there's no point in just waiting indefinitely for somebody to claim it, because if they don't claim it soon they never will. But even if I should have to keep it, I wouldn't keep it for myself or spend it on myself. I wouldn't feel right doing that, even if I knew no one would *ever* claim it. I just never would feel it was my money to do that with. What I might do, though, is just let it go against Papa's doctor bills. Practically charity, you might say. That would be the thing to do with it. Not use it selfishly to buy something for myself—though God knows I could use it—but just let Papa get the benefit of it without ever knowing. Poor old soul. Well, maybe that's why I was the one that found it—on account of Papa, and us being so dreadfully hard up these days. Maybe I ought not to even worry my head about it at all, because the Lord *does* bless us in devious ways. Lot of people would look at it that way I'm sure. But no, I don't want to start that. I mustn't try to talk myself into that money because it's not mine. Not yet it isn't. I've got to wait several days at least and see if it's claimed.

I'd return it in two minutes, if I knew whose it was. I honestly believe I would. In fact, I know I would. Because I could never bring myself to keep money, even found money, that belonged to somebody else and I knew whose it was. I've never done a dishonest thing in my life. I've got to stop worrying about it, though. I've had it on my mind ever since it happened, and there's no point in fretting myself sick about it. I don't know why I'm making such an issue of it anyway. All I can do is just wait, and if somebody claims it, well, I'll just have to give it up, that's all. I'll be more than glad to. But I do wish I could get it off my mind awhile, I've got to think of something else. What about supper?—there's something. What can we eat for supper? I'm not the least bit hungry, and that's a fact. I'm too tired to eat. And I don't want to have to wash dishes the way my ankles are killing me tonight. I just don't think I could stand it. Well, let's see. There's some beans and turnip greens and one piece of tenderloin left over from dinner. I could eat that. That would be a plenty for me. Papa will want some Cream of Wheat, I guess, and maybe that'll be enough for him tonight. I can give him a glass of buttermilk if he wants it. He shouldn't eat much at supper anyhow, that's why he don't sleep any better than he does. Dr. Clemmons said not let him eat hardly anything before bed. Which reminds me. I've *got* to send Dr. Clemmons a check. I've *got* to, even if we're overdrawn. If no one claims that purse, won't *that* be a blessing? Now I'm back on that again. Well, all I can say is, whoever it belongs to can gladly have it. All they've got to do is identify themself. If that's dishonest in any way, I'm badly fooled.

She sighed and shook her head, going painfully up the steps to her house. As she opened the door, her father called to her. "That you, Elsie?"

"Yes, it's me, Papa." It could be no one else, not today nor tomorrow nor any other day for as long as the two of them had left on earth. She turned on the hall light, put down her purse and the books she had brought home, and went straight into his room. The old man was sitting up in bed with the county paper spread open across his lap.

"I see here by the paper where Miz Morris Walker lost a pocketbook with some money in it. It don't say how much. She's offering a ten-dollar re-ward; says they was a key in it she wants the finder to return, no questions ast."

Elsie Cotter looked at her father lying there fat and sick and old, with pipe ashes all over the bedcovers, and for one brilliant instant she wanted to choke him. You meddlesome old fool! she wanted to shout. You've fixed it now, and I was only doing it for you!

She went quickly into the bathroom and closed the door, and hot tears of anger stung her eyes—anger at him, but also at herself. Mainly at herself. Her, a Morgan, rationalizing that way, lying to herself so she could steal. A Morgan stealing. My God, she thought. Have we come to this, finally? Stealing? What has the world got against us that we have to be pushed down and down and down till nobody even remembers who we are or what we've been. Don't they know this town was *named* for my family? What have I done to deserve this? Why do I have to be punished with this poverty, and this filthy, ignorant old man my mother never, never should have married in the first place? What *is* it? What in God's name have *I* done?

And think of that fat hussy saying it was the key she wanted back. The *key*, mind you. Sitting up there so high and mighty in a big fine house and two generations ago they were sharecroppers. Yes, sharecroppers. Oh, I know you all right, Miss High-and-mighty Walker, I know all about you. Your great-grandfather was run out of the county over a Nigra girl, and you had an uncle who died drunk on the public square. The key, eh? No, the money doesn't matter does it? Just the key. Just because the Fairchilds and the Byjohns and a few more have taken you in, you think you're *so* high and mighty. And those Brayleys, too. Think of it. Living up there on Sycamore Hill where the Morgans belong—where *I* belong. That clan living in the old Morgan house. Sharecroppers, carpetbaggers, bootleggers! Yes, go ahead and say it, she thought, because it's true. All right. Nigger-hoppers! That's what you are, all of you, not two generations ago!

She put her face in her hands and cried.

2

When the three of them, Harper, Dill and Preacher, returned to their room they pulled down the shades, locked the door, and Harper got out a pencil and a large piece of brown wrapping paper. He pulled a chair up to the dresser, and sitting there with his legs spread awkwardly apart because there was no place to put them under the dresser, he began to draw a diagram on the brown paper. "I'm going to show you what I mean," he said. "It would be a good idea for both of you to memorize this."

Preacher had brought a sack of apples back to the room with him, and while Harper was drawing, he stretched out on his bed to eat one of them. He had a sharp knife, and he peeled the apple carefully, letting the long spiraling peel hang down from the blade as he went around the apple.

"I don't know if I can take it in here with all the shades

down," Dill said. "I can't breathe in here. I swear if it's a hotter hole in the forty-eight states I'd like to know about it."

"Take your shirt off," Harper said. "Strip down and you'll get cool."

Dill took off his coat, and then his shirt and tie. He wanted to take his trousers off too, but Preacher was watching him, getting ready to make some remark about his underwear again, so he left them on. He lit a cigar and sat down by the window so the little draft of air that came around the edge of the shade would hit his back.

They were silent for a while as Harper continued to draw. Preacher ate his apple, cutting off neat crescent-shaped wedges and lifting them to his mouth with the point of the knife. Dill watched him with distaste. When he had finished the apple he tossed the core across the room at the wastebasket, but he missed it and the core rolled under the dresser. He adjusted his hearing aid, opened the sack, took out another apple and began to peel it slowly, carefully in the same way.

"You going to eat another one?" Dill asked.

"That's right."

"What's the matter, didn't you get enough to eat at supper?"

"I like a little dessert," Preacher said. "Apples are one of my favorite desserts."

"So I see. How many you planning to eat?"

"Oh, I don't know. I may eat the whole sack, if I feel like it. It's nothing to you."

"I didn't say it was anything to me. Eat as many as you want."

"I will."

"All right, you guys," Harper said.

"All I ast him was if he meant to eat another apple," Dill said. "He's got to give everything a smart answer."

"Let it lie," Harper said. "I'm trying to concentrate."

Dill continued to watch Preacher as he peeled the apple. He was fascinated by the way the knife went smoothly around it, curling off the long, continuous strip of rind.

"What's the matter?" Preacher said. "You ever see somebody peel a apple before?"

"I seen hogs eating apples once," Dill said. "You'd be right at home with a bunch of hogs, eating about a hundred goddam apples at a time."

31

"Two apples. You call that a hundred? You must not can count either, Dill."

"I can count."

"All right, for God sakes," Harper said. "You guys act like a couple of kids. Try and get along for a change, will you? This is important."

"All I ast him was if he meant to eat another apple."

"And I told you," Preacher said.

Harper got up and spread the big piece of brown paper on the bed. "Here it is," he said. "Get up, Preacher, or at least move your feet. This is the bank."

Preacher swung his legs over the side and sat up, and Dill crossed the room to stand beside Harper. They looked down at the diagram, and Harper began to talk, pointing at the paper with his pencil.

"This here's the door, of course, and like I told you, the cages run along the right side here where you see these squares. Back here there's two or three desks that belong to the cashier and I guess the president or vice president or whoever he is."

"What's that, a wall?" Preacher said.

"No, it's one of these little fencelike affairs. Just about waist high. We got a break on that. You can see the whole bank the minute you step in the door. The vault is here, in the back wall, and as far as I can tell, it stays open all day."

"No offices in the back?" Dill said.

"No offices anywhere. All the desks sit right along back here behind this little fence. You can see the whole bank and everybody in it the minute you step in the door. The only place there could be somebody we don't see is in the john."

"That's just our luck though," Dill said. "Just about two minutes before we go in, some bastard is going to take a notion to take a whiz probably."

"How many in there?" Preacher asked.

"Six. I counted them three times to make sure. And three of them are women."

"I don't like those women in there," Dill said. "A woman can always start screaming her head off."

"You ever see a bank without a woman, Dill?"

"No."

"All right, then. It happens to be one of the hazards in a deal like this. I don't think we'll have any trouble though. They're insured, and nobody is going to get very brave about some cash that's already insured. We're all right. They'll line up nice enough."

"And you're sure there's no alarm?" Preacher said.

"Absolutely positive. Not even a guard. That's one of the reasons we picked here to start with."

"Okay," Dill said. "Go ahead."

"Well, now about the safe. The vault door is a Mosler, and it's my guess that the safe is a Mosler too. From where I stood, it looked like a regular two-and-a-half-inch screw, three-phase delay lock—and incidentally, it was standing wide open the whole time I was in the bank."

"No crap. You could see the money?"

"No, but I could see the safe door all right, and it was standing wide open. If our information is right, there's anywhere from seventy to eighty thousand in it, just waiting to be lifted out. However, we can't count too strong on the safe being open. They rig those things for fifteen minutes at a time, during banking hours, so if we happened to hit it wrong we might have about a fifteen-minute wait."

"I don't think my nerves could take it," Dill said.

"They'll take it. They'll have to take it, if things break that way. That's why we're waiting till five minutes till three to go in. We'll draw the blinds and just sweat it out—nobody on the outside will get suspicious. The bank's closed as far as they know. Their watch is slow. And here's something else to remember. If anybody tries the door, don't lose our head, see? It's just somebody trying to make the bank before it closes. We just sit tight. His watch is wrong. Understand?

Dill and Preacher nodded.

"Now. There's plenty of silver back there—ten thousand or so probably—stacked all over the place. But that stays, understand? We don't touch the silver, even if we get no more than five dollars from the safe. It's just too damn heavy to fool with when you're in a hurry. You two ought to know that by now, but I don't want anybody getting any last-minute ideas about grabbing himself a bonus."

"What about the back door?" Preacher said.

"No back door. That's tough, but that's how it is. We come out the same way we went in."

"I don't like that," Dill said.

"But listen," Harper said. "Here's the main thing of all. We got to be in that bank at five minutes till three. If we run a minute late we're out of luck, because at three sharp they're going to screw up the safe door and it won't open again for God Himself till nine o'clock Monday morning. Got that? If we're as much as two minutes late, the whole thing's off. Is that *clear?*"

"That's clear."

"All right. Now, about the car. It looks like we'll have to grab a car."

Dill began to shake his head vigorously. "Not me. I don't take no car. I told you, Harper. Nothing doing. That's the surest way in hell to get messed up before you even get started."

"Now, wait a minute," Harper said. "I'll get the car myself. Don't worry about the car. All you have to do is stop some guy at the corner and get in. That will happen around two, so we'll have plenty of time to get rid of him and get back to town."

"I don't like it," Dill said. "You start fooling around like that and you'll have the heat on you before you ever get to the damn bank. I swear to God, Harper. I told you to check on the car."

"Can I help it if this is a hick town? How am I to know you can't even rent a goddam car?"

"You're suppose to know."

"I said forget the car. I'll handle it, and I guaran-dam-tee you it'll go off like silk."

"You're getting ready to kill somebody is what you're getting ready to do."

"Nobody gets hurt. Jesus Christ, Dill, if I can't heist a car by this time I'll quit!"

"What will you do with him?"

"Who, the guy's car we take? We just tie him up good and dump him somewhere. By the time they find him we'll be long gone."

"All right, you handle it then. But I'll tell you one thing. If there's any hitch about the car, Dill is out, see? Dill don't even know you."

"Shut up, Dill," Preacher said.

Harper sighed and mopped his face with a handkerchief. "All right," he said. "We go in at five minutes till three. That means we got to have this hick Law out of town by two forty-five or fifty. Dill, we'll give you that to do, if it's not asking too much. All you do is you go in a drugstore, phone the police and say there's a car wreck on highway eleven, ten miles north of town. Lot of people killed. Got that?"

"I got it."

"Those boys should be leaving town just about five minutes before we pull up at the bank, so make sure of your timing."

"Don't worry about my timing. You just time that car."

"What about the shotgun?" Preacher said. "We can't get in there with a shotgun, can we?"

"I don't know," Harper said. "Maybe we'll leave that out after all. A big gun like that throws a nice scare in them, but it's hard to manage without you're wearing a overcoat. I don't know. Maybe we'll just leave it out. Leave it at the truck with Slick."

"That Slick is somebody else I'm worried about," Dill said. "I wish we had us a white man on the truck."

"Slick's all right," Preacher said. "I'm more worried about *you* than anybody, myself."

"By the way, when is he due in?" Dill said, ignoring Preacher.

"Not till tomorrow," Harper said. "We can't afford to have anybody see him or the truck, I don't want him in town at all."

"Memphis, here I come," Preacher said. He stretched out on his bed again and straightened the wire of his hearing aid. "Eighty thousand squid. Man, won't it rock this little jerk-water town?"

"Think of them that's in the bank, though," Dill said, smiling a little for the first time. "Won't they do some talking? You know, it's a funny thing when you stop and think about it. Here we are getting ready to dish up some real excitement for these farmers and they don't dream a thing about it. Some of them are going to be in that bank when we walk in tomorrow—just in there by chance probably—and look what happens. They got something to talk about the rest of their stupid life." He looked at Harper and grinned.

"That reminds me," Harper said. "There's a phone back there in the vault. So if there's somebody in the vault when we go in, wait till they come out before you start anything. that's one way they might cross us up."

"Check," Preacher said.

"Funny thing though," Dill said. "You plan the hell out of something like this, but you never can be sure how it'll come out. It's the only thing that worries me. I tell you the truth, I don't believe I could shoot a man to save my life."

"Me neither," Preacher said.

They both looked at him and he gave a high soft giggle.

3

At nine o'clock the kids were in bed and Shelley and his wife were sitting on the screened porch. They had left the light off, so as not to attract mosquitoes, and Shelley had opened a couple of beers for them, which they were drinking from the cans, sipping slowly and talking in the dark. Helen was smoking a cigarette.

"You won't believe it," she said, "but this is the fourth cigarette I've had all day. I had one after breakfast and two this afternoon while Jimmy was asleep, and now this is number four. I actually don't have time to sit down and drink a cup of coffee and have a cigarette any more."

"What's the matter, the kids give you a hard time?"

"Days like today they do. That Jimmy. Honestly, Shelley, he's more trouble than both the girls put together."

Shelley sipped his beer and smiled. "Turn him over to me when he gets too rough. I'll tan his rear for him."

"Look who's talking. Shelley, you wouldn't lay a hand on that boy for all the tea in China. Besides he's too little to spank. Who ever heard of spanking one ten months old?"

"I'll spank him. I'll straighten that young gentleman out."

"Yeah. I can just see it. You're what's the matter with him now, the way you pamper him."

"Well, I got a big interest in him. Look how hard I had to work for that boy."

"Shelley Martin. You ought to be ashamed."

Shelley laughed and sipped his beer in the dark. Heat lightning played along the horizon.

"I wonder what Dave and Sue are up to tonight," Helen said. "We should have called and had them come over for a beer."

"I didn't think of it," Shelley said. "I haven't seen Dave in I guess it's a week now."

"Sue was over this morning to help me fit a dress. She don't look well either, Sue don't. She ought to see a doctor about that digestion of hers."

"What's the matter with her digestion?"

"Nothing agrees with her. She told me today she can't even drink a cup of coffee without it giving her heartburn. I think she's got an ulcer, myself."

"Heartburn don't sound like an ulcer. With an ulcer you have the stomach-ache. There was a boy in my outfit overseas that had an ulcer. He used to get the stomach-ache all the time; had to keep eating all during the day. Every time his stomach got empty, bingo, he'd have the stomach-ache. You get an ulcer and you know it, all right. You don't have to wonder what's wrong with you."

"What causes an ulcer anyway?"

"Nervousness mainly," Shelley said. "Take when we were flying a lot, this guy used to have the stomach-ache all the time, whether he ate or not."

"I don't see why they could put somebody like that in the Army in the first place."

"Too much liquor can give you ulcer too," Shelley said. "All these big whisky drinkers show up with ulcer before it's over."

"That Boyd Fairchild's certainly due for one, then. And his wife too, from what I hear. They say those two drink like a fish practically every night of the world."

"That reminds me," Shelley said. "Me and Boyd are going fishing tomorrow afternoon. I'll have to have the car."

"What's the matter with *his* car?"

"I don't know. Maybe his wife needs it. Anyway, he asked me to come by for him."

"Needs it for what, I'd like to ask. To run after somebody else's husband with?"

"All right, Helen, just leave that to the rest of the blabbermouths. You don't know a thing on earth about Emily Fairchild, and it will pay you to leave that kind of talk to somebody else. Don't forget, I work for the Fairchilds."

"I know you work for the Fairchilds. I'm just telling you what I hear."

"And another thing. Boyd Fairchild is all right. He's been mighty nice to both of us, and we owe it to him not to repeat what every Tom, Dick and Harry has to say about him."

"I'm not criticizing Boyd. What did I say about Boyd?"

"You said he drank like a fish, for one thing."

"Well, he does, Shelley. You know that as well as I do. Everybody knows it. He doesn't even pretend not to, for God's sake."

"And what's so wrong about drinking?"

"Oh forget it. I don't want to fuss."

"I'm not fussing," Shelley said. "I'm just telling you. What the Fairchilds do is the Fairchilds' business. If they want to get lit every night of the week it's nothing to us."

"Well, I'll stand by Boyd. Boyd's all right. But I don't have to like that wife of his. And I'll tell you something else, too. You don't like her yourself, Shelley. Tell the truth. Do you like her?"

"I don't *hate* her."

"Just say if you honestly and truly like her. Tell the truth. How would you like it say if they lived next door and she was dropping in over here like Ann does, or Sue? How would that suit you?"

"I wouldn't care for that, sure. But that's carrying it to the extreme. I still say what she does is her own business, and we'll do well to keep our nose out of it. She's not bothering us."

"Isn't she?"

Shelley looked around sharply in the dark. "Just what was meant by *that* remark?"

"Nothing, Shelley. Don't blow up."

"No, I'm serious. Just exactly what are you driving at?"

"All right. I suppose she never made a pass at you."

"She certainly has not."

"Are you right sure, Shelley?"

"Of course I'm sure. Goddam it, Helen, what's the matter with you? Do you think I'd even look twice at Boyd Fairchild's

38

wife? Are you accusing me of trying to pull off something like that with three children in there and as good a job as I've got? What's the matter with you women anyway? I swear, I'm a son of a bitch if I ever heard anything to beat it!"

Helen put her head back and laughed. Then she got up and came over to the glider. She bent down and kissed him softly on the ear. "I'm only kidding, baby," she said. "Cool your little fevered brow and don't get so upset. Mamma's only teasing."

Shelley sighed and shook his head. "Christ Amighty, you women. Here. Get me another beer before I break your big fat neck."

"Shelley Martin!"

"Your slender, pretty little neck, then."

"That's better." She took his empty can and started back into the house. "Can I have another one too?"

"Yes, you can have another one too."

When she was gone, Shelley sat in the dark and looked out through the screen at the lights along Baird Drive. Two houses away some people were sitting on a lighted screened porch, like his own, playing cards. Now and then they would all laugh and lean forward in their chairs; then they would lean back again and the sound of their voices would die away. A car passed, and a moment later a boy on a bicycle went around the corner in front of the Methodist church. He was whistling. "The Stars and Stripes Forever," and there was some sort of a band instrument in the basket of his bike.

Helen returned, handed Shelley a frosty can, and sat down beside him on the glider. He put his arm around her and let his hand rest against her breast.

"Shelley, do you really think I'm getting too fat?"

"No, I was kidding, hon, you know that."

"I mean really. What's the old saying—'Many a true word is said in jest'?"

"I was only kidding, so help me. I wouldn't want you to lose an ounce."

"*I* think I'm getting too fat. I'm getting too hippy. Haven't you noticed how hippy I'm getting?"

"I've noticed you've got some hips on you, but hell, a woman's supposed to have hips. You want to look like one of these scrawny little girls in the fashion magazines? They look to me like they've all got TB. I like a woman to have some hips on her." He let his hand down and slapped her solidly on the thigh. "None of these hipless wonders for me."

"Emily Fairchild's got a nice pair of hips on her."

"Yeah, but nothing above. I bet old Boyd wouldn't know what a nice pair looks like."

"Still, she's got a neat little figure. You can't take that away from her."

"I don't want to take it away from her."

"What about it, Shelley? Don't you think she's got a bedroomy look about her?"

"Listen, *Damn* Emily Fairchild. Will you please get Emily Fairchild off your brain. I wouldn't touch that hen with a ten-foot pole and you know it."

"I know it, Shelley. I'm sorry. Not another word about her. Let's talk about me and my big fat hips."

"Not big fat hips at all. Nice, full, just-right hips." He kissed her cheek.

"And about my big, strong, good-looking man."

"Cheap flattery will get you nowhere."

"Shelley, where'd you hear that."

"Hear what?"

"What you just said, about cheap flattery will get you nowhere."

"What makes you think I heard it somewhere?"

"Because it don't sound like you. It's not the kind of thing you'd make up in your head. I'll bet a hundred dollars you heard somebody else say that first."

Shelley laughed. "I read it in a magazine," he said. "I read it in a story in *The Saturday Evening Post*."

"I thought so. A remark like that is no more like something you'd say than anything in the world. It's just not the way you'd say something—'cheap flattery will get you nowhere.' Shelley, I know you so well you couldn't fool me in a million years, you know that? I know you so darn well. If I was blind, I'd know you in your sleep, just by the way you breathe. I know you, Shelley." She turned her face up to him and he kissed her. "Shelley, I know you like I hope no other girl in the world ever has or ever will."

"Listen," Shelley said. "When you kiss me like that I feel as though I had just lost an engine on take-off."

She drew back and looked at him. "Where did that one come from?"

"Same place. A story I was reading in the *Post*."

"Honest to God, Shelley. What makes you read that tripe?"

"I like it."

"I believe you do. Well, you don't talk to me like that, mister. You know how I like to be talked to."

"How do you like to be talked to?"

"You know."

"Like this?" He buried his face in her hair and whispered something into her ear.

"Shelley Martin!" She giggled and closed her eyes. "Yes, that's it though. I'm awful, I guess, but Lord I love it."

"Look out," he said. "You're going to spill your beer."

4

Down at the Blue Moon, Frank Dupree was having a cup of coffee and talking to Sybil the waitress.

"Well, the social lights are really throwing one tonight," he said.

"Yeah? Who's that?"

"The young social lights. Boyd Fairchild and the Brayleys and that crowd. They're all drunk as glory out at the golf club."

"Is that so?" Sybil was a big girl with a wart in her left eyebrow. She was leaning against the back counter, picking her teeth with a match.

"I've carried three fifths out there already."

"You don't say. Old Kelley's really raking the money, eh?"

"Ten bucks a fifth," Frank said. "But money don't mean nothing to that bunch, I swear it don't. The Byjohn boy give me a five-dollar tip the last trip I made. Just like that. 'Here, Frank,' he says. 'Here's a little something for yourself.' "

Sybil shook her head. "Well, you know the saying about a fool and his money."

"That's the gospel truth, and as long as they're throwing it

41

away I might as well get it as the next fellow. They got plenty of it to throw."

"I cain't take that bunch," Sybil said. "They're a little too snotty to suit me. Especially the women. Especially certain ones of them."

"Well, it's money. You get money, you can afford to act like a horse's rear and get away with it. Boyd Fairchild ain't a bad fellow though."

"No, he's all right. And that Parks boy, in fact both of the Parks boys. But some of those wives. No thanks."

Frank sipped his coffee and looked at himself in the mirror of the cigarette machine which stood at the end of the counter. "I had a fare this afternoon that's got me puzzled," he said.

"Yeah? Who's that?"

"I don't know. That's what has me puzzled. These three birds come in on the Memphis train. Said they was with the TVA, but I'd bet dollars to doughnuts they wasn't."

"What makes you think so?"

"I don't know. They never looked right somehow."

"Well, that's the world for you," Sybil said philosophically. "People always putting on the dog, trying to act like they're you-know-what on a stick."

"That's a fact."

Mrs. Carrington, Emily Fairchild's mother, was having a cup of hot chocolate before bed, and Judge Carrington was reading a paperback novel called *Murder Goes Naked*. The Judge had taken his shoes off, and Mrs. Carrington was studying him thoughtfully as she sipped her hot chocolate.

"John dear," she said, "do you think we could get dogwood to grow out there at the end of the drive under the box elders?"

The Judge looked up. "I suppose so. Why?"

"I was just thinking, we need something along there to fill in that space, and dogwood is so pretty in the spring."

"Yes, I think it would grow there all right." He returned to his book.

"What about quince? Flowering quince."

He looked up again. "Quince? I doubt it. Too much shade. Dogwood is better."

"When does it bloom?"

"Dogwood?"

"No, quince."

"February, isn't it? We had a bush there by the chimney once, don't you remember? I think it used to bloom in February."

"What time of year do you transplant dogwood?"

"That I don't know dear. You'll have to ask Mac or someone. Mac could tell you." He raised his book again.

There was another question Mrs. Carrington wanted to ask, but she let it go. She didn't want to disturb his reading again.

In the club car of the Dixie Flyer Mr. B. J. Fairchild was talking to a major from Fort Sill, Oklahoma, who said he was on his way home to a funeral.

"My sister's husband died," he explained, "and I'm going back to help out till things are cleared up a little."

"Any children?" Mr. Fairchild inquired. They were drinking Tom Collinses.

"No, fortunately, no children."

"I don't know if I'd call that fortunate or not," Mr. Fairchild said mildly. "It's fortunate in one sense, of course, but I imagine your sister will be sorry not to have had children. They can be a great comfort, you know."

"Yes, you're quite right," the major said. "In one sense, I see your point."

"Will you have another drink?"

"I believe I will, thanks. But this one will have to be on me."

"Not at all," Mr. Fairchild said. "I always like to treat the man in uniform. I was in the service myself once, and I always enjoy talking to you fellows."

"What was your outfit?"

"I was in the Fifth Division during World War One—the old Red Diamond."

"Oh yes," the major said. "Well, the Army has changed a lot since those days, I'm afraid."

"My son served in the Navy during the last one," Mr. Fairchild said.

Chapter Four

To most of their mutual friends, Boyd and Emily Fairchild were an unlikely match. They both were attractive—

nobody denied that—but what seemed unlikely was that they should have married each other. The odds had been against it all the way. For one thing, they were the same age and they had grown up together, and men seldom marry the girls they grow up with. Long friendships, especially those begun before puberty, engender a fraternal attitude in the male; and though it was natural enough that Boyd's first date should have been with little Emily Carrington who lived next door, it was really surprising that he finally ended up by marrying her. Another thing that made it an unlikely marriage was the fact that both their families had been strong for it from the first.

The simple truth of the matter was that Boyd and Emily loved each other. They fell in love as soon as they were able, and stayed that way; and the natural order of things went out of balance. It would have been all right, too, except for one thing, and that was Emily's disposition. She had a wild, reckless streak in her. She loved Boyd probably as much as he loved her, but she was impulsive and unstable. She had a tendency to "carry on," as the Negroes put it. Mrs. Carrington blamed it on the fact that Emily was a premature baby. "Premature children are always nervous children," she said. "They start life at a disadvantage and they never quite get over it." Emily's father was not so sure. His own secret conviction was that they had spoiled Emily, raising her as an only child, giving her everything she wanted, letting her have her way always, even in the smallest matters. If there had been other children it would have been a different story, he thought, but there were no other children and that was that.

Actually, Judge Carrington did not understand his daughter at all, and neither did his wife. The only person who really understood Emily was Boyd. In moments of exasperation he was fond of saying, "I don't understand you, Emily," but he did. Even the unpredictable things were predictable to him. He had learned to expect the unexpected, and he had conditioned himself to a life of paradox. He knew, for instance, that the strongest bond between them was Emily's infidelity to him. He knew that their longest single step toward each other had been made, paradoxically, on a night when Emily spent four hours in a Charlottesville tourist cabin with a fraternity brother of his. He knew Emily and he knew how she felt and how to handle her. She was sorry and ashamed when she came back to him that night; all he had to do was forgive her. It had cost him something, but then life with Emily was more a matter of giving than receiving, anyway. He knew she loved him, no matter how often she betrayed him, and that knowledge was what held their marriage together, because it was all that really mattered to Boyd. Only when he was drunk did he forget this, or ignore it, and he was always sorry afterward. If it was a weakness to look at it that way—to think that her love was worth what it cost him—well, then he was a weakling. But he could not imagine another kind of life, without her.

He knew Emily. He could read her like a book. He knew, for instance, that she had been unfaithful to him again in the second year of their marriage when she went away to Atlanta to attend the wedding of a friend. He did not know who the man was or how or exactly where it had happened, but he knew it *had* happened, as soon as she came back. She loved him too tenderly. She was too solicitous. It was all right. He was sorry and he was glad. That was life with Emily. A going away and a coming back, and the coming backs were what renewed and revitalized their love.

It gave him pride, though, to know that she had never violated their marriage with any of the men in Morgan. Most people thought she had, but she hadn't He knew this. And secretly he thanked her for it.

The main trouble now was the question of children. Boyd wanted children and Emily did not. She still felt young, she said (she was twenty-seven), and she wanted to enjoy life a little longer. She had seen how tied down you can get when you start having babies. Boyd knew, though. Emily was afraid. The thought of child-birth frightened her. Well, all right, he told himself. Someday it will happen anyhow, and you'll see it was worth it. Most things that are worth while in life cost you something.

As for Emily, she was a puzzle to herself. There was a chronic restlessness in her, that much she recognized, but where it came from, or why, she couldn't begin to guess. "What's the matter with me?" she often asked herself. "Why

45

do I do these things?" Then, without waiting for an answer, she would try to think of something else. Most of the things she did seemed pointless, even when she did them, and even when she enjoyed them. Life either excited her or bored her, and there was no in-between. But it was all pointless anyway. The only steady certainty in her whole existence was Boyd and her love for him; her infidelity was the greatest puzzle of all, the greatest source of frustration and remorse. She loved him alternately with tenderness and passion, but she loved him best when he was not looking—at a bridge game as he studied the dummy hand, or at a party when he stood across the room talking to someone else. She loved him best, always, in the moments of unawareness—especially when he was asleep. Sometimes when he was asleep she would look at him and imagine that he was dead, and the most exquisite and perplexing sense of guilt would come over her, almost as though she had killed him.

Together they were an attractive and popular, if unlikely, couple. They had an expensive new home and plenty of money; in the summers they played golf and swam and occasionally took a trip; in the winters they shot quail and played bridge and went to football games out of town. They had friends in Memphis and Atlanta, and they were probably the best liked, best envied couple in Morgan. They were good dancers, good talkers and good drinkers, and they had a natural air of ease and sophistication that came from knowing they were the upper crust of the upper crust in Morgan, Alabama. They had been brought up in old homes, where there were cherry corner cupboards and sugar chests, and crystal that had come down the French Broad River and survived the Civil War.

2

By ten-thirty the party which had begun at the golf club at five o'clock that afternoon had moved back to town and into a little modern glass house owned by Jack and Martha Byjohn. A few had dropped out along the way, but others had taken their places and now there were six couples and three or four stags, all going strong. Things were getting pretty drunk. In the kitchen, Dink Hartman, wearing an old rubber fishing boot on his head, was reciting "The Cremation of Sam McGee"; and Wally Faulk, the dentist, who had joined the party as late as eight o'clock, was already so drunk he had locked himself in the bathroom and couldn't get out. A dice game had started behind the breakfast bar, and Eileen Eubanks was going into a lot of detail about her hysterectomy. Boyd Fairchild and Emily were in the living room with Jack Byjohn and the Pete Brayleys, listening to some old Benny Goodman records that Jack played only on special occasions, like tonight. Nell Harriman was still remarking to people that the best parties were always those that started without anybody planning them, and people were still agreeing with her on it.

"I'll tell you one thing, though," Pete Brayley said. "We got to get old Wally out of the toilet. He's been in there over an hour now."

"He's all right," Jack Byjohn said. "He can't hurt anything in there."

"Yeah, but I'd like to have a crack at it myself," Pete said. "He's been monopolizing that thing for an hour. He must think we're all a bunch of camels or something."

Pete's wife sniggered over the rim of her glass. "You don't mean camels, honey. Camels are what can go without drinking so long. You mean something else."

"I know what I mean. I mean there's no sense in him holding up the deal like this every time we have a party. He does it every damn time. What's the matter with that guy anyhow? He's a real toilet hound, ain't he?"

"I don't think he wants to get out," Emily said.

"Yeah, he wants out all right," said Martha Byjohn. "I went out there awhile ago and I could hear him monkeying with the latch. You see, the trouble is the latch on that door is kind of tricky. You have to hold up on the knob to make it work."

"Well, why didn't you tell him," Jack said. "He probably wants out as bad as we want in."

"I *tried* to tell him, dear, but he's so tight I don't think he understood. Anyhow, with all this racket."

"Listen to this," Jack said, putting on a new record. "I want you to just listen to this Teddy Wilson on this side. I swear that guy is a real master."

47

"Well, I'm going out there and see if I can get that bird out of the toilet," Pete said. "If I don't, I've got to go home."

"Aw, look at the big baby," his wife said, and giggled again. "Look, folks, he's liable to wet his breeches any minute."

"Laugh all you want to, but I'm getting sick and tired of that tooth-puller locking himself up in the can every time he gets two drinks in him. Hell, you can't enjoy a party if you got to sit around with your legs tied in a knot all night."

"Go ahead, get him out, then."

"I'll give you a hand, Pete," Boyd said.

"Wait just a minute," Jack said. "I want you to catch this Wilson. I swear this guy is a master."

"Never mind Wilson," Pete said. "Wilson can wait."

He and Boyd got up and walked out in the hall where they found Dink Hartman, still with the boot on his head, stooping down to peep through the keyhole.

"What's he doing in there, Dink?"

"I can't even see him," Dink said. "He must be in the closet."

"Here, lemme take a look," Boyd said. He bent down, swaying slightly, and looked through the keyhole. "I see something that looks like his sleeve," he said. "I believe he's right up here by the door."

Pete cocked his head against the door. "Wally? Can you hear me?"

"Wassa matter?" a voice said from the other side of the door.

"Say, Wally, how about coming on out?" Pete said.

There was no answer.

"Hey, Wally!"

"Wassa matter?"

"Listen," Pete said. "You gotta open the door, Wally. Come on out and give somebody else a break."

"Listen, Wally," Boyd said. "Hold up on the knob and the latch will work all right. Just raise up on the knob and at the same time push back the latch."

"Wassa matter?" Wally said.

"Christ Amighty," said Pete. "Wassa matter, wassa matter—is that all that halfwit can say? Does he think this is funny or what?"

"Let me try," Dink said. He addressed the door. "Hey, Wal, how about opening up, old trooper? I got you nice bourbon and water mixed up out here. All you got to do is come right on out and get it."

Suddenly there was a loud, resonant bumping noise within the bathroom. Dink pressed his eye to the keyhole. "Well, I'm a son of a gun. Hey, Wally! You all right in there? Wally!"

There was another muted commotion. "Wassa matter, you guys?" Wally said.

"I'm going home," Pete said. "By God, I'm going *home*.

In the meantime, Bill Clayton had come into the living room and asked Emily to dance.

"I don't want to dance," she told him. "What do you want to dance with me for?"

"I just thought we'd dance," he said helplessly. "What's wrong with that? Every time I've opened my mouth today you've jumped down my throat."

"Oh, go away. You bore me. I know what you're thinking, Bill Clayton."

"You do, eh? Well, for once you're wrong," he said angrily. "I don't know what's got into you lately, but I'll tell you one thing. It's not on *my* mind anything like as much as it must be on yours."

"I bet! Why don't you get married? Why don't you stop horsing around with everybody else's wife for a change?"

He looked at her a little closer and saw what he had not noticed before: that she was drunk. Good and drunk. She could fool you sometimes because she didn't get that blank look that most of them got. But she was drunk now, all right, and that called for a change of strategy.

"Look," he said, "if I apologize and call a truce, will you stop being sore at me?"

"I'm not sore at you. I'm bored at you."

"All right, but will you accept my apology? I'm sorry I asked you to dance. I'm sorry I ever even looked at you twice. Very sorry, Emily. And if you really want to know why I don't get married—well, I'll tell you someday. You ought to know, though, without being told."

A queer look crossed her face. "What kind of a line is *that*? Why should *I* know why you don't get married?"

He gave her a feeble smile and walked sadly away toward the kitchen. She followed him in, even before he had time to pour himself another drink.

"Just exactly what are you driving at, Bill Clayton?"

"Nothing, Emily, just forget it. I never should have brought it up in the first place." He turned away, as if to hear the story Ed Harriman was telling.

"No, I'm not going to forget it, either," Emily said. "Bill, you're not . . . I hope you're not trying to say you're in *love* with me, for God's sake."

She had said it a little too loud, and Bill looked around uneasily, but everyone was occupied, talking and laughing—no one had heard her. He turned to her again and gazed at her steadily. "I promised myself you would never know, Emily, but I guess I've let the cat out of the bag, haven't I?"

"I think you're giving me a load of bull, Bill Clayton."

"Okay, then skip it then," he said. "It can't make any difference now anyway. Can it?"

"No. Bill, you're not serious, surely."

"I told you to forget it. Just forget the whole thing, Emily. Just say I'm drunk and don't give it a second thought."

"Bill—"

"Consider the matter closed and forgotten." He started to walk away, but she caught his arm.

"What is it, Emily?"

"I think you're giving me a big line of crap."

He shrugged and started away again.

"Well, I'm sorry I talked like I did to you in the car."

He smiled at her forgivingly.

"I am really. I'm sorry as hell. I've been sorry all night. It's spoiled the whole party."

"Well," he said, "you're sorry, I'm sorry. Now let's have another drink and forget the whole mess."

"But I don't want to forget it; I think it's perfeckly awful. But my Lord, Bill, *I* didn't know. You never said anything."

"What could I say? After all, you're a happily married woman and . . ."

"Don't be too sure about that."

Oh, *brother*, he thought. "Emily, let's not talk about it any more. Not in here, anyway. Somebody might hear us and you

50

know how they all are. They practically think we're having an affair already." Use of the word "affair" had been a risk, but he wanted to see what effect it would have on her.

"Let's have that drink you offered me," Emily said.

"How you like that guy?" Pete Brayley said. "Did you ever hear anything to equal it? I swear, I'm going to get him outa there if I have to call the Fire Department."

"No need for violence," Boyd said. "Just stand back and let old Fairchild han'le it. I've han'led these things before." He drained his highball glass and set it carefully on the floor against the wall. He rubbed his hands together and licked his lips. "All right, Wally. Now, look here, old boy. Wally?"

"Wassa matter, you guys?"

"Listen, Wally. Listen with all your might. *Open the goddam door.* Hold up on the knob and just push back as easy as you can on the old latch, watcha say?"

"No."

"Well," Dink said, "least we got a new answer that time."

"What'd I tell you?" Pete said. "That simpleton, he don't want out. Why, damn his soul, we oughta break in the door. How you like that? One hour and fifteen minutes!"

"Look, Dink," Boyd said, "will you please open the door?"

"I'm Dink," Dink said. "That's Wally in there, remember?"

"Right you are. I meant Wally. Wally, come on out and act like a human being."

No answer.

"Well, that settles it," Pete said. He turned and walked down the hall and disappeared into the living room. After a moment they saw him come out again and walk stiffly toward the door with his hat on backward. He looked very much offended.

"Wait a minute, Dink," Boyd said. "Where's my wife?"

"I don't know," Dink said. "I haven't got the dimmest idea." He went into the kitchen, and Boyd was left alone in the hall, standing by the locked bathroom door.

"Wally?"

There was no answer.

He went down the hall and into the kitchen, looking for Emily. She was not in the kitchen, so he went into the living room. She was not there either.

"Listen to this one, Boyd," Jack said. " 'Please Don't Talk About Me When I'm Gone.' "

"Wait a minute, I'm looking for somebody."

"Who? Emily?"

"Yeah." But he wasn't. He was looking for Bill Clayton now.

Chapter Five

They must be some kinda Law, Sugarfoot told himself. They got to be. They must be these guv'munt agents, G-men, or some other kinda Law.

He didn't believe it, because they didn't look like the Law; but for four hours now, ever since discovering the gun in the suitcase, Sugar had determinedly evaded the truth. Ain't but two kinda people tote guns, he told himself. Law and outlaw. They got to be the Law. It won't do to look at it no other way.

Lord, Lord, I got me a mess now though. What I got to go nosing around up there for in the first place?

I declare, a man's nose may get him in more trouble than his organ. How come I cain't set down here like I'm suppose to, 'stead of prowling around upstairs going through everybody's suitcase and hunting up some kinda gun. Man, I ought to have my head examine for doing something like that. Now look at me. I got me a mess sure enough. Got that man's gun in mind *all* night long. Cain't even rest. Done swallowed down a whole bottle like it was no more than branch water, and look at me. Setting here a hour till quitting, just as cold, flesh-crawling sober as I can be. Seem like if I much as shut my eyes, first thing I see is somebody with a gret big gun in something. I neen think I'll rest tonight. They bound to be some kinda Law though. It won't do to look at it no other way.

Sugarfoot was alone in the lobby. The lights had been turned off everywhere except at the desk and at the doorway, and the shadows seemed to be encroaching on the wide hall itself. Sugar moved his chair closer to the open door to get a cool air and to hear the occasional sound of a car that told him he was not entirely alone in the night. Miss Benson was not in yet; if it weren't for her, he'd close on up and go to bed. No one would know the difference. He longed for another drink. Just a small one, he thought. Something to go to bed on.

He thought of the three men upstairs in 201 and a chilling idea came back to him: suppose they planning to hold this place up tonight. Ain't I in some fix though? Gret God, they liable to shoot old Sugar down in cold blood. He shook his head. they won't mess with no chicken feed like us, not them three. Anyhow, they most likely some kinda Law, down here to check up on something. Just the same, if Miss Benson don't put in her appearance before long, I may just close on up and try to get me a night's rest. I could leave the door unlatched so she can get in by herself. I declare it makes me uneasy to think about a gun in a *suit*case. What would a man put a gun in a suitcase for? Unlessen he meant to hide it. Don't seem like a man would do a thing like that. If he was a guv'munt agent though. You take a guv'munt agent, he got to shake it around right queerly in order to nab these crim'nals. Most likely they under orders of some kind. My, my, don't I need me one though? I liable not sleep a wink for that gun. I know one thing, if I go to dreaming about somebody with a gun in a satchel I ain't going to rest well at all. I never did like a gun in a suitcase. Seem so underhanded. I cain't make out what them three doing here anyhow. Naw man, I ain't seen nothing of that style around here before.

If they was to come down them stairs right now and go to robbing this place, I declare ain't a thing on earth I could do to stop them. I ain't even armed. I'm a unarmed man. Best thing for me to do in a case like that is just haul ass. Naw man, I ain't able to stop them. Best thing for me to do is just talk to them dogs, right through the door and on down the street. I mean *leave* here. They ain't nothing like that liable to happen though. It would of done happen if it was going to, I guess. I ought to be armed though, keeping this late desk ever night. I must speak to Mr. Neff tomorrow. Right now I'm just as unarmed as I can be.

Maybe I ought to told Mr. Neff. He ought to known about that gun before bed. Naw, on the other hand, it wouldn't done no good. If they is the Law it's all right, and if they ain't the Law it won't do to provoke them. A man with a gun in a suitcase don't take much to provoke either. He liable to lose his head and go to shooting. Best let a sleeping dog lay. That's right.

Besides, I done stuck my nose too far in the hole already. I be better off not knowing half I already know. Lord, don't I wish I could mine my own business though? A man ought to have his head examine.

The water cooler at the end of the hall clicked on and Sugar jumped out of his chair. When he heard the hum of the motor he sat down again and sighed with relief.

Man, I sure do need a little something to study my nerves. Mercy.

2

"Don't start the car," Emily said. "We can talk right here all right."

"What if somebody comes out and sees us? You know what they're going to think, don't you?"

"Never mind what they think. Besides, it would be much worse if we disappeared somewhere. You know that. If we leave, then they will have something to talk about."

"Okay, we'll stay here, then. But I don't know why you bothered to come out at all, if this is all we're going to do, just sit here in front of the house."

"Just what *do* you think I came out for?"

"Well, you said to talk."

She sipped her drink and shook her head. "You were the one that said that. You said we couldn't talk inside."

"All right, *I* said it, then. But we still can't just sit here like this."

"Why not?"

"Well, because."

"Because why?"

"Oh, Jesus Christ, Emily, are you trying to drive me nuts? *You* know what I mean; we can't just sit here in front of the house. Any minute somebody's liable to come out and see us here."

"Well, so *what*? We're only talking, aren't we? Is there anything wrong with us sitting out here and talking?"

"Frankly, yes. And you know it."

"Yeah, I suppose so. What did we come out here for, anyhow?"

"You tell me."

"To neck?"

"Emily, don't be so damn *broad* always. You can drive a man out of his mind."

"Well, that is what we came out for, isn't it? At least, I'm beginning to think that's what *you* came out for. Where's all that love talk you were giving me in the house?"

"Look, Emily, put the drink down, won't you? You're getting way too much, baby, no fooling."

"I'll decide how much I can drink and how much I can't, Bill Clayton. All I want you to decide is what you brought me out here for."

"We came out to talk." Bill took a handkerchief from his pocket and mopped his brow. "We came out to talk and get a few things straightened out. But you don't seem to want to, all of a sudden."

"What do we want to get straightened out? If I don't miss my guess, you've already got something straightened out. But it won't do you any good. Not tonight it won't."

"Emily, for God sakes."

"All right, so we came out to talk. You said that. You started a lot of high-powered stuff in the house there about being in love with me; but I'm beginning to have my serious doubts. You may be in love, all right, but I'd hate to say what part of me it's with."

"Emily. Look, baby, don't drink any more, please,"

"Come to the point," she said. "What are we supposed to be talking about, love or just plain old sex? Tell the truth now, don't give me the run-around."

"Emily, I can't talk to you when you're like this. Let's take a little ride in the cool air. It'll do you good and then we can talk all we want to."

"You make that word sound like something else."

"Will you?"

"Will I what?"

"Go for a little ride."

"No. I told you three times. What do you think I am, a

whore? I can't jump in the car and run off with you, and Boyd in there. Even if I wanted to."

"You could tell him you had a headache and ask me to drive you home."

"Yeah. He'd be sure to believe that."

"We wouldn't be gone long."

She looked at him curiously. "You know what's the matter with you, Bill? You're adolescent. Pubescent. You can't grow up, can you?"

"Emily, don't drink that. Let me finish it for you. You've had too much, baby."

"No, and stop calling me baby. I'm not your baby; I'm Boyd's baby."

"All right."

"All right what? You brought me out here you said to talk. Well, let's hear it. I've got to go inside pretty soon."

"Okay, here it is." He took a quick look toward the house, then pulled her to him and kissed her. She let him, not resisting, not responding, but being careful to hold her drink out so it would not spill.

"Well," she said. "Now that we've talked, I better go back to the house."

"No, wait a minute. Why do you act like this?" He pulled her back and kissed her again and put his hand between her legs.

"Stop, Bill."

"No."

"Bill, will you please *stop* that?"

He embraced her, trying to kiss her again, but she resisted, turning her head from side to side. They struggled quietly in the dark; then she got her hand free, spilling her drink, and slapped him solidly across the jaw.

There was a moment of total silence.

"Now look what you've done," she said. "You've made me spill my drink all over the car."

"All right," he said. He reached across her and opened the door. "Get out. Go on get out, you little bat."

"Don't tell *me* to get out."

"You heard me."

They stared at each other in the dark.

"All right," she said. "I'll get out. You're damn right I will. I'll be only too glad to get out."

"Do it, then!"

She opened the door and slammed it resoundingly behind her. Then she turned and stuck her head inside again. "So you're in love with me, eh? I see. Well, you can go straight to hell, you nasty-minded jerk!"

"Go away," he said. "Go on in the house, you drunken bat."

"You go on, too," she yelled. "Go on home and suck your thumb; it's the best you'll ever do!"

When she was halfway up the walk she heard Bill Clayton's car scratch angrily away from the curb and bump one fender against the light pole, and in the same instant she saw the front door open. She stopped and stood where she was until she saw that it was Pete Brayley. Pete had his hat on backward and he looked pretty tight. She didn't care if Pete saw her, and she decided to speak to him; but Pete didn't even look up. He was in a huff about something. He angled unsteadily across the sloping lawn and disappeared into the night.

I better go in the back door, Emily thought. Boyd is probably beating the bushes for me by now.

She walked along the side of the house, looking in the windows, and around to the back porch. No one was in sight, so she opened the screen door and went into the kitchen where a dozen or more people were laughing and talking loudly. The first person she saw was Boyd. He was standing alone in the hall, between the kitchen and the dining room, and he was looking directly at her. He'd seen her come in the back door, but that was all right too. He hadn't seen Bill Clayton—had not seen her *with* Bill Clayton, at least. She gave him an equivocal smile and leaned over the breakfast bar to watch the crap game now being played by Ed Harriman and Fred Eubanks, but out of the tail of her eye she was still watching Boyd. He was coming toward her down the hall, looking a little belligerent. When he reached her elbow, he said quietly, "Mind telling me where you've been?"

She looked at him with surprise, then leaned over the bar

again. "What do you mean, where've I've been? I've been out in the back yard."

"With who?"

"With *whom*, darling."

"All right, with whom, then."

"With myself. I needed some air."

"Bill Clayton must have needed some too."

"Really? I wouldn't know about that."

"He was with you."

"No, he wasn't."

"That's a lie."

She turned and looked straight at him, noticing for the first time that she couldn't quite focus her eyes. "Look," she said, "if you want to call me a liar, wait till we're home, will you? I'd rather our friends didn't know."

"Come out on the porch."

"All right."

He walked grimly ahead of her, bumping the door frame with his shoulder as he went through.

"Now," he said, when they were alone on the porch. "What kind of a deal are you trying to pull off?"

"Nothing."

"Zat so." He was swaying a little as he looked at her. "Well, listen, I happen to know Clayton was out there with you."

"Out where?"

"In the back yard."

"He most certainly was not. If you insist on knowing, Boyd, I went out there because I had to go to the bathroom and that stupid Wally has everybody locked out."

"I don't believe it."

"All right, don't. I don't give a damn."

"Did you, Emily? I mean, was that all you were doing? Bill wasn't out there at all?"

"Bill Clayton went home hours ago, Boyd. You must be drunk."

"Don't lie to me, Emily."

"Boyd." She took his arms and pulled them around her. "Baby, don't accuse me of things like that. You know I couldn't be unfaithful to you if I tried."

"I don't know," he said. "God knows I don't want to believe it, Em."

"Of course you don't. And you mustn't either, because it makes us say bad things to each other. Things we're sorry for tomorrow. Come on now, kiss and make up."

He kissed her. "You want to go home?"

"In a little while."

"I'd like to go home now, I don't feel so good."

"You poor baby." She brushed his hair back from his forehead and leaned against him. "You and me've both had too much drinkie, baby, you know that? Look at us, we're waving around all over the place."

"I'm drunk. I didn't mean to either. You're sure about Bill Clayton? He wasn't out there?"

"I told you, Boyd, I went out in the yard to piss."

"Emily, I don't like for you to talk like that. I wish you wouldn't do it. When you get like this you always start talking ugly. Vulgar talk. What makes you do it?"

"I dunno." She had her arms around him, her head against his chest, swaying slowly to the music that issued from deep in the house. "I honestly don't know what makes me do it, Boyd. I've got a common streak in me, I guess. It comes out, don't it?"

"Just when you're tight like this. I wish you wouldn't though. It sounds like hell to hear a pretty girl saying some of the words you'll say."

She giggled and snuggled closer to him. "Dance with me, baby. Come on, you're not dancing."

"Promise me you'll watch the language?"

"I'll watch it, I promise. Don't you want to dance?"

He set his glass on a chair and they danced.

"Better?"

"Much better, bunny man. Ooooo, things going round and around."

"Maybe we ought to stop."

"No, don't stop, you're my bunny man. Am I your baby, Boyd?"

"Yes, baby."

"Nobody else's?"

"Nobody else's at all."

"And you love me good? All of me?"

"I really do."

"I love you too, Boyd. I may be a bad girl, but one thing I do, I love you. I want you to remember that forever and ever."

"I will."

"Listen," she said. "Was that thunder?"

"I didn't hear anything."

"I did. I thought it was thunder."

"If it's going to rain, maybe we ought to head for home."

"Yes, let's go home," Emily said. "I don't want it to rain."

3

I'm insane, Harry Reeves told himself. That's what's the matter with me; I've lost my mind. I belong in an institution somewhere.

Harry was hiding behind a tree on Barker Street, near Fenton's used-car lot, and by looking down the narrow dirt street that ran behind the Commerce Hotel, he could see all the windows along the rear of that building. He was watching one window in particular, but it was dark like all the others.

Harry's friends would scarcely have recognized him if they had seen him there. Instead of his usual dark business suit and white shirt, he was wearing an old cotton jersey and a pair of paint-smeared jeans. A brand-new black sateen baseball cap was on his head, and instead of the conservative, bulbous-toed shoes he usually wore at the bank, he had on sneakers. He was in disguise. Dressed for sin, he told himself bitterly. Costumed for the vilest depravity. His hands shook; he cried a little and blew his nose, looking up and down the dark street. What's the matter with me? he thought. I am insane. Just as sure as anything I've lost my mind. I'll kill myself.

He looked at his watch and pulled the bill of the cap down lower over his eyes. The lights of a car swept the corner behind him and he flattened himself against the tree, heart pounding. Caught, he thought. No, they're going the other way. Thank God for that. He peered around the tree and saw the taillights disappering. I will be caught, though. Sooner or later I'm bound to be. I can't go on like this. Look at me. Peeping around trees like an idiot. I'm insane, all right. I belong in an institution. But I don't care. I don't *care*. I can't help it. God knows I can't help it. I don't know *what's* got into me. Fifty-five years old and doing a thing like this. A family man, respected, trusted, a deacon in the church; now look at me. A Peeping Tom. Yes, go on and face it, because that's all I've become, a Peeping Tom. I should be locked up somewhere away from decent people. But I don't care. I swear I don't care if I suffer in hell for it eternally. I can't help it. Oh my god, I can't help it.

He cried again and blew his nose, watching the rear of the hotel.

Harry Reeves' ordeal had begun just three weeks ago, although when he thought back on it, it seemed an eternity ago. One night as he was walking home from a Civitan meeting he had taken a shortcut behind the hotel, and accidentally had seen Miss Benson undressed in her room. It wasn't intentional; it was the most innocent thing in the world. He just happened to glance up and there she was. She was washing out some stockings in the basin. He just glanced up, not even thinking what he was doing, and there she stood revealed from the knees up in the open window, wearing nothing but her step-ins and a brassiere. He looked away quickly and walked on down the street toward home, but in that glance, in that split second of surprise, something terrible had happened to him. He did not sleep well that night, even though he embraced his wife; and all the next morning the memory of that lighted window kept drifting to the surface of his thoughts.

At noon of the next day as he was walking home to lunch, he saw Miss Benson come out of the five-and-dime store wearing her white nurse's uniform and carrying a large paper parcel. He was walking fast and would have overtaken her in half a block, but instead he slowed his step and stayed behind, watching. He fed his eyes on the motion of her hips straining the white poplin skirt as she walked, and the deft switching back and forth of the hem of her skirt above the seams of her stockings. It filled him with desire, and he had to look away from time to time, drawing deep breaths of the hot summer air.

He told himself then that he must be careful. He must not allow himself to think such thoughts. But that night at nine o'clock he discovered that he was out of cigarettes, and he walked to the drugstore for a pack, taking the shortcut behind the hotel. He was disappointed this time, however. There was no light in Miss Benson's room and actually he was glad, he told himself. But when he reached the drugstore he hung around for a while, drinking Coke (which he ordinarily never did at night because they kept him awake), and when he started back home again he walked slowly along the street behind the hotel, looking at the window. When he passed the window and was near the corner of Barker Street, he remembered that he probably needed some razor blades too, and he walked back a second time to the drugstore. But even then, passing the window for the fourth time that night, he saw nothing. Miss Benson was out on a date and would not be in till midnight or so, and there was no excuse to invent that would keep him out that late.

For more than a week he stayed off the street behind the hotel, walking scrupulously down the square and going half a block out of his way to get home. During that time he saw Miss Benson only once, and she was in a car then, so his eyes were not tempted. But he could not forget, and finally, on one particularly sultry sinful Thursday night, he told his wife he'd left some work at the bank, and he set out with no other thought in mind than to see Miss Benson again without her clothes on. I'll do it just this once, he told himself, and then maybe I'll get over this vulgar infatuation. I'll go and I'll look at her, naked if possible, and that will purge me. I'll disgust myself, and then I'll be over it for good.

He walked down the little street behind the hotel that Thursday night and when he saw Miss Benson's window he stepped into the shadows to wait. It was a long wait too, because Miss Benson was a late reader, and this time she was sitting fully dressed under a bridge lamp, reading as if she had no intention of ever going to bed. Ironically, she was eating a bunch of grapes—the one fruit Harry Reeves detested. But Harry was patient, he had come to purge himself, and at last his vigil was rewarded. Standing there in the shadows, his pulse pounding and his breath coming in hot, shallow gasps, he saw Miss Benson in her most intimate nakedness. She was a little knock-kneed, and for some reason he could not name, that fired him to a frenzy of desire. He stumbled home feeling sick and debilitated, and tears filled his eyes. He knew his trouble was not over; it had only begun. He had not been purged at all. The very next day he bought the black sateen baseball cap and the sneakers, surrendering himself utterly to sin and vileness.

Now, as he stood behind a tree on Barker Street waiting for Miss Benson's light to come on, he wondered for the hundredth time why in God's name she didn't pull down the shade and release him from this bondage. Why, he thought, doesn't she stop me? All she has to do is draw the shade and then I *must* be cured. If I knew, postively *knew* that I couldn't see her I'd be all right. It's this knowing I can that overpowers me. It's lying there and knowing that all I have to do is come down here and wait.

In his dozen-odd trips to the street behind the hotel, Reeves had seen Miss Benson draw the shade only twice, and on one of those occasions it was not pulled all the way down. Her failure to take that simple precaution seemed to him a symptom of loose-minded indifference—a lewd indifference. It wasn't that she didn't think to do it; she just didn't care. The nights were hot, and with the shades up it was a little cooler, so she left them up. If someone saw her undressed, well, the hell with it. That was her attitude. Actually, there were no buildings directly behind the hotel, only vacant lots and back yards, and therefore a small likelihood that someone would see her; but still, she mainly just didn't care. Because she must realize the chance that someone could come along the back street and see her. No, she just didn't *care*, that was it. Like the knock-knees, this regardlessness only served to heighten Reeves' desire—and he didn't know why.

He looked at his watch again and moaned. It was after midnight and still no sign of her. She's out with that Kelley again, he thought. No telling where they go or what they do. God in heaven, I do envy that man. He probably does anything he wants to her. Think of that. Think of those naked legs, think of them kissing like that, and oh my God just *think*. He shook his head. I'm insane, all right. I belong in an institution, locked up somewhere away from decent people that have decent thoughts. I'll kill myself. That's what I ought to do is kill myself, I'm not fit to live. His eyes filled with tears.

Look at me, he thought. I cry all the time. I'm an emotional wreck. I'm not myself any more, not myself at all. They ought to send me away somewhere. Really. I'm not fooling anybody, either. Why don't I admit it? I'll bet a thousand dollars everybody in town is talking about me—how I follow her in the street, how I've lost so much weight and everything. For all I know, someone may have seen me down here peeping on her. Those men at the filling station; I bet they just sit there and laugh at me. Oh, I'm crazy, all right. I'm completely out of my mind and I'd be better off dead. If my mother could see me now. I'll pay for it, too. God is testing me, and I haven't the strength to face the test. I wish they'd send me away and forget about me. I wish someone would run over me with a car. I wish I was dead. He cried and sniffled and blew his nose.

Suddenly he saw a flicker of lightning in the southwest and then, a moment later, heard the threatening mutter of thunder. Now look what's happening, he thought. A storm is coming up and here I am. What if the thunder wakes Mildred and she goes in my room? What excuse can I tell her? I went out for a walk because I couldn't sleep? She'd never believe a lie like that. I think she's suspicious anyway. She's seen the way I've lost weight and how nervous. Oh Lord, please don't let it rain. Don't make me go home yet. I've waited so long. Send her to me. Let her come home now and let that light turn on up there and let me see, see, *see* . .

4

In room 201 it was quiet, except for Preacher's thin, sibilant snoring and the occasional rustling of the window shade as the breeze pushed it out and let it fall again against the window. The window of that room faced north, and the lightning flashes were visible only as pale reflections against the sky.

"Harp, you awake?" Dill whispered.

"Yeah."

"I'm sorry I blew up about the car."

"It's okay. I didn't take it to heart."

"Well, I shouldn't have blew up, anyway."

"Forget it."

Dill rolled over and inched up to the edge of his bed. "I cain't sleep, can you? Listen at that bastard snoring."

"I wish he'd turn on his stomach," Harper said. "It's when you sleep on your back that makes you snore."

"Think we could turn him?"

"No, we'd just wake him up."

"I doubt it. Honest to God, that guy's just a little *too* cool to suit me. Listen at that, will you? Sleeping like a baby and I can't shut my eyes. We ought to screw that thing in his ear and let him help us listen."

"You're not scared, are you?"

"Naw, just nervous. You know how it is. You're awake too."

"I've got a headache," Harper said.

They listened to Preacher's snoring and Dill gave a long weary sigh. "I'll tell you that guy gets me, Harp. I'm awful afraid we made a mistake bringing him along."

"No, we didn't. We need him. And you know why."

"I know, but still, don't he kinda give you the creeps sometimes? That voice of his."

Harper said nothing.

"They named him right, all right. Preacher. He *looks* like a damn preacher. That's what gives me the creeps. He looks like a damn undertaker."

"Look at that," Harper said. "You see that lightning?"

"Yeah, I been noticing it for half an hour. Seems to be a storm coming up."

"Maybe not."

"I wish it would. Cool things off. I'm sweating like a nigger writing a letter. Couldn't you use a little cool air?"

"It would help, that's a fact."

"I hope it rains like a bastard," Dill said.

Harper rolled over to face him. He was sleeping in his underwear and lying on top of the covers. Dill could see his gold wrist watch in the faint light from the window. "You know," Harper said, "I hadn't thought about it before, but a rainy day might be a break for us."

"How's that?"

"Well, you know how it is when it rains. Visibility is cut down. Everybody's windshields gets rain on it, and people stay indoors more. We're not as likely to have somebody get a good look at us."

"Hell, everybody in town has already seen us."

"No, I mean leaving the bank. Which way we went, and that sort of thing."

"Maybe so," Dill said. "I mainly just need some cool air. I haven't been able to draw my breath hardly since we hit this place. But you know something? I don't believe it bothers that Preach a bit. Nothing bothers that guy, does it?"

"Not much."

"I think he's nuts, Harp, no crap. I never run across one like him before. I mean he's really mean, that sucker is."

"He's a cold fish, all right."

"He's mean. I wouldn't trust him as far as I could throw a wet mattress.

Harper laughed. He was lighting a cigarette. "Don't worry," he said. "Long as he's on our side we're all right."

There was a long silence, punctuated by Preacher's snoring. Dill rubbed his feet together and sighed again nervously. He wanted to talk.

"Talk about mean, though, there's nothing in this world as mean as a goddam mean-ass woman, you know that? I been lying here thinking, all the things that's happened to me over women. They can ruin you, you know that? And mean? A man cain't come anywhere near a woman when comes to being plain low-down."

Harper said nothing. He didn't want to get Dill started.

"I had me a wife once—you remember Paralee, don't you? When we lived in K.C.?"

"Yeah, I met her once."

"Now, there was a woman for you. When I first married her I thought I'd made a haul. She was on the skinny side, of course, but I always liked them a little that way for some reason. Most men like a plump woman, but I was never that way. I thought I was in clover for a while there, even took a job and went straight over her." He raised himself on one elbow and looked at Harper in the dark. "You know what that broad did? Ran off with a goddam wop. No crap. She left me for a wop."

He lay back again and looked up at the ceiling. "To tell you the truth though, I was about halfway glad to see her go by that time. She had a lot of little habits that used to get on my nerves. I don't look it, but I'm a nervous sort of a guy, and sometimes

66

she would really get on your nerves. All of them are that way. You live with one awhile and you find out the moon ain't made of green cheese after all. This Paralee, she had a habit of going around all day in a housecoat. She practically lived in the damn thing. I was running book for Blackie Johnson out there then, and I used to come in home around four or five in the afternoon and find her still laying around there in a housecoat. She was lazy, was what it was. After breakfast the first thing she'd do was fall up there on her butt on the couch, and many's the time I'd come home and still find the breakfast dishes on the table. Things like that."

"Yeah," Harper said.

"But the worse thing was the way she always had this cold. All winter long with a cold. Sniff, sniff, sniff—you ever see a woman like that? I swear to God, even when I think of her now, I can hear that sniffing going on. Then about every two weeks she'd give the damn thing to me, of course, and here we'd go. I swear I never got as tired of anything in my life as I did of those colds she used to have. Whenever I still see somebody with a cold I always think, oh-oh, Paralee. It's the first thing that pops in my head. She was the world champion when it came to a goddam cold. A little thing like that don't sound like much, but it can get you down after so long a time."

"Sure it can," Harper said. He was smoking, not listening.

"Then there was something else—and this will hand you a laugh, but I'll tell you it wasn't funny at the time. You see, I'm a guy who likes his vegetables cooked fairly dry. That's why I don't go for this Southern-fried business—too greasy. I like my vegetables just boiled or steamed or something like that, but not all this grease. Well, Paralee was a grease maniac. Everything she cooked had to be floating in goddam grease. I know this sounds silly, but a little thing like that can work on you after a while. Every day the same thing: vegetables floating in a lot of grease. Grease running all over your plate, getting on your bread and your meat and every-damn-thing. Well, I tried to be patient, see? I'd say to her, 'Look, honey, I don't go for all this grease on my food. How about when you dip up my beans, take and drain off about half of that juice.' All right. Next meal, same goddam thing. Just one great big pool of grease. Bread, meat, potatoes, everything, *drowned* in it."

Harper closed his eyes and shook with laughter. He could see that, all right. Dill trying to be patient over the grease.

"Then there was this brother she had," Dill went on. "You hear a lot of jokes and all about brother-in-laws, but it's a fact, some of them can get to be a real pain. This character was a hotshot, or so he thought. He was only about nineteen or twenty, but he knew it all, see? Oh, he was wise. He had him one of these Olds convertibles and he had it all niggered-up with spotlights and sun shades and a million other gadgets. He used to look like a goddam appliance store coming down the road in it, no crap. I can see him now. Even inside he had it all niggered-up. You couldn't hardly see through the windshield for all these fuzzy dolls and things that he had won at a fair somewhere. He had them hanging on strings all over the windshield, and all that stuff jittering around in front of your eyes when you were trying to drive. I never drove it but once though. But he thought it was great; he had a lot of wise talk, and he used to slay the women. He thought. He used to bring these little pimply-faced girls around from the bowling alley and snow them under with a lot a big talk. They always had on slacks. But the thing that really used to kill me was the way Paralee couldn't see through him. Loan him money any time he ast for it. I kicked his tail out, finally, and in a way that was what broke us up, although I think she was already fooling around with the wop. I don't know. He was a barber."

"Who the brother?"

"No, the wop."

5

The storm woke Shelley when it broke, and when he switched on the night light beside the bed, Helen woke up too.

"What's the matter, Shelley, are we having a storm?"

"Yeah, a little thundershower, I guess. I thought I better check the windows."

"See about the kids too, will you?"

He got up and walked barefoot through the dark rooms, feeling the window sills to see if it was raining in, and pulling down most of the windows on the south side where the wind was hitting the house. It had rained in a good bit in the kitchen; there was water all along the shelf above the sink, and he even felt some on the linoleum, cold and unpleasant to his bare feet. Now and then there would be a flash of lightning which showed the curtains ballooning at the windows, and then a long rending sound of thunder, like the splitting of some tremendous green oak board, followed by a heavy concussion. The wind was blowing hard too, lashing the rain over the roof. As he went back to the bedroom he heard the lid fly off the garbage can and go rattling across the yard.

"There went the garbage can," Helen said. "We're having a pretty bad storm, aren't we?" She was looking at him over her shoulder with the sheet pulled up to her chin—looking sleepy and alarmed at the same time.

"It's not too bad. Just a thunderstorm. I imagine the farmers are glad to see it."

They were silent for a while, listening.

"How long is it since we had rain?" Helen said. "It seems like a year ago."

"The second week of June was the last rain you could call a rain. And this is what? July seventh or eighth."

"Eighth. I know because I wrote the grocery check today. Listen to that wind."

"Well, it ought to cool things off awhile anyway." He sat down on the edge of the bed and reached for his cigarettes on the night table.

"You going to smoke?"

"Yeah, I'm wide awake now. Want one?"

"No thanks."

They listened to the storm. The thunder crashed and lightning flickered, making brilliant stripes in the Venetian blind.

"Some wind, all right," Shelley said. "I wonder if it'll blow down Parker's TV aerial again."

"I wonder. It looks to me like they'd all blow down, the way they run them up there so high on those skinny little poles. We ought to have us a TV, Shelley."

"Yeah, I know it. I'm going to talk to Harry about one the first chance I get."

"The kids would love it so."

"It's educational too, in a way. Just so you don't let it interfere with their school work."

They listened again to the commotion of wind and rain. Helen rolled over and reached behind him for the cigarettes.

"I was just thinking," she said, "how times have changed, just within my memory. Television for instance. Lord, when I was a kid nobody ever heard of television, and now practically every house you see has a TV sticking up over the roof."

"What about jet planes?"

"Yeah, and not to mention atom bombs and hydrogen bombs. But Lord, look at us, sitting up here at one o'clock in the morning talking about jet planes and atom bombs like it was the middle of the day. I'm wide awake now, though. The storm, I guess."

"It's slackening off already," Shelley said. "Notice that wind? It's slackened off a lot."

Helen sat up in bed and pulled her knees up, tucking the sheet around them. "There's something about a storm, isn't there? I like to be in bed when there's a storm."

"I just thought of something," Shelley said. "This is liable to knock my fishing trip in the head tomorrow."

"Oh, it probably won't rain long."

"I don't know. I've seen it set in like this and rain a solid week after drought."

"Well, I hope not. Listen. Was that Jimmy?"

"Yeah, I'm afraid it was." He got up and tiptoed to the bedroom door, listening.

"Was it him?"

"I think so. I hear him flopping around in his crib."

"Damn. It was the thunder that woke him. I was afraid of that." She threw the sheet back and started to get up.

"I'll take him," Shelley said. "You just stay in bed. I'm wide awake, and, besides, I can sleep in the morning."

"I imagine he'll doze off again if you rock him. Don't you want me to take him?"

"No, I'll go in; you stay in bed."

Shelley took a last drag on his cigarette and mashed it out in the base of a flower vase that stood on the chest of drawers. As he went down the hall he heard the child begin to cry loudly.

"Hurry, Shelley," Helen said. "Before he wakes up the girls."

70

Shelley switched on the hall light as he went by, and coming into the room saw the little boy standing up on his knees in the crib. His eyes were shut tight and he was not completely awake yet, but he was distressed and frightened. Shelley picked him up and began to walk back and forth, talking to him soothingly.

"All right, Jimmy. All right, boy. Daddy's got him. Don't be afraid. Daddy's got this boy."

The little boy sniffled and buried his face against Shelley's neck. Shelley rocked him slowly from side to side as he walked up and down the room. After a few minutes the child relaxed again, going limp in his arms, and Shelley knew he was asleep; but since the storm was still howling at the windows, he continued to walk, waiting until the noise had subsided before putting him down. He felt the child's soft cheek against his, the little back no wider than your hand. Lord, they are helpless little things, he thought. I guess that's why you feel this way about them. He walked back and forth. When they grow up it's not the same, I guess. I don't see how it could be. I don't know though. Maybe it is the same, just on a different scale or something.

He patted the child gently, rocking him as he walked. You feel so damn protective, he thought. Don't be afraid, you tell them. Daddy's here and everything is all right. Daddy will even stop the thunder and the rain for you. He smiled to himself and shook his head. I don't know, he thought. Sometimes it scares you, don't it? Think of all that's ahead of them. Makes a man wish he really could protect them, all the way. But you can't do that though. It's the wrong attitude to take. You just tell them don't be afraid, and then you go right on being a little afraid yourself. I wonder if other people feel that way. Like in the morning, for instance—always, just when you wake up and think well here's another day, and you have a queer sort of scared little feeling for a minute or two. And like what Helen said about being in bed when there's a storm. I wonder what it is that makes a man want to be in bed sometimes, asleep, and don't want to wake up. I got nothing to be afraid of. No more than the average fellow anyway. There's something though you never are quite sure of. Like you'd forgot something important and can't remember what it was. What's the word I want? *Vulnerable*, I guess it is. A kind of vulnerable feeling, especially at night, and when you first wake up. You pick up the paper and there's a riot in Syria, or somebody has shot at the ambassador or the Reds are acting up again. All that kind of stuff for breakfast. And yet most of the time that don't really worry you much. If they blew up the whole goddam world with an atom bomb it couldn't kill you but once. It's something else. Something a lot closer to home, but still you can't put your finger on it. Like you had forgot something important before you went to bed. I don't know. Maybe I've still got a touch of war nerves or something. It's not that though, because I remember it even when I was a kid. I guess it's just human nature. A little feeling that somewhere, somehow, something is wrong. You don't know what it is yourself, so all you can tell the kids is just don't be afraid. That's all. But we're all afraid, I guess. Scared of the dark.

The storm had subsided now and a gentle rain was falling from the vast sudden stillness of the night. Shelley put the child down gently in the crib and patted his back. "There, boy," he whispered when the child stirred. "Go to sleep, Jimmy. Daddy's right here with you, boy. Nothing to be afraid of. Nothing at all."

PART TWO

Chapter Six

If anybody in the world ever needed a drink, it was Sugarfoot. Here it was just about dawn of day, raining, and him lying there wide awake and tight as a banjo string from the calves of his legs to the back of his neck. There was a wild, empty feeling in his stomach too.

I got to have me one sure enough this morning, he told himself. I made the biggest mistake of my life not going on last night and buying me another bottle before bed. I ought to known better than try that. Now look at me.

He got up shakily and looked out on the wet street behind the hotel. Sugar's room was on the ground floor of the hotel—a converted supply closet, actually, no more than seven feet wide and with only the one window which had been cut out of the wall after Sugar moved in and had never even been painted. The facing and sash were still unpainted after twelve years. Sugar looked out the window and tried to estimate what time it was. About five, he thought. Between four-thirty and five. He knew there'd be no one in the kitchen yet, so he dressed hurriedly, sighing and shaking his head, and stepped out into the back hall. No one in sight. Walking on his tiptoes and trembling a little in the legs, he made his way to the kitchen and from there to the door of the pantry which was in an alcove to the right of the dining-room entrance. The pantry door was locked, and that was the one key Sugar didn't have on his ring, but he didn't let that stop him. Taking out his pocket knife, he opened the blade and slipped it between the edge of the door and the jamb. When he felt the point against the tongue of the lock he pressed it back and the door opened nicely. The vanilla extract was on the third shelf of the right wall, stacked alongside the nutmeg, bayleaf and paprika. There were eight

73

bottles standing in two rows of four, one behind the other, and Sugar was careful to take a bottle from the back row so that the shortage would not be immediately detected. He might even replace the bottle before it was missed. This was the sort of thing he hated to have to do, because even *Mister* Neff objected to this; but in an emergency a man had to make use of whatever resources were available to him.

Sugar put the bottle in the pocket of his white jacket and closed the door, hearing the lock click into place again. He was already feeling better, because the bottle was in his pocket. To need a drink and have one ready is not so bad; it's when you need one and haven't got it anywhere in sight that's hard on the nerves. He didn't waste any time though. He stopped at the water cooler, made sure no one was around, and drained the little bottle in two swallows. It went down his throat and into his stomach sweet and hot—so hot, in fact, that he could trace the course of it all the way down and into his intestines. His eyes watered, his throat constricted, and for a minute he thought he was going to lose it; but he bent over the fountain and drank some water and pretty soon everything was all right. The heat of it warmed him to the bone, a tingling warm pleasantness spreading all over inside him; and then came the fine feeling of assurance. Everything was all right now, hunky-dory. At least till he could get over to the poolroom and buy him another bottle of popskull.

It was still early and he debated going back to bed, but decided against it. I might sleep off my buzz, he thought, and I sure don't want to do that. For one thing, that poolroom don't open till eight o'clock, and I'll be pushing it some to stay limber till then. I cain't go in that pantry no more, not today I cain't. I got to make that little extrack last till way up in the day. Man, I sure ought to went over there and got me another one before bed last night. But I'm all right now, long as I don't eat too much breakfast and bury this buzz I got on.

He went up the hall to the lobby, walking steady and sure of himself now, and suppressing a little chuckle. Always after a good swig took hold of him he felt like laughing, though he didn't know why. It was like a funny secret when you had a good stiff one under you, and sometimes it was all he could do to keep from laughing out loud. It made everything so fine, nothing to worry you. He could feel it creep up on him now, fuzzing him up and making the soles of his feet tingle. Gret God, he thought, that small bottle done hit me like a ton of bricks. Must be my stomach was empty. I declare I believe a man could just go on and on. You cain't do that though. It don't pay to abuse your drinks.

Standing at the lobby windows, looking at the rain falling on the early morning streets and the wide deserted courthouse lawn, he thought of the men up in 201 again. Well, I let that gun throw a scare in me, he thought, but I musta been right all along. They some kinda Law. Bound to be now, because if they had any mischief in mind I imagine we'd of heard about it by now. They been here ever since yesterday evening and ain't nothing happened yet. I guess I was right, all right. Of course, they don't look like the Law, but then the Law don't always look like itself. Sometime they got to act strangely to nab these crim'nals. I imagine what they down here for is on account of this bootlegging. They liable to be after Mister Ace Kelley, for all I know. Wouldn't that be a shame though if they was to arrest Mister Ace? I sure hope they don't. That could put us in a strain sure enough, if a man had nowhere to go to get him a bottle. We might have to go back to making homebrew. Mercy.

Thinking of Mister Ace had put him in mind of Miss Benson again, and he remembered a strange thing that had happened in the night. It was one o'clock when Miss Benson came in from her date, just a minute or two before the storm broke. Sugar had already given up and gone to bed, but when he heard her come in and go up the stairs, he had gone out to the lobby in his stocking feet to latch the door. When he returned to his room and started to get back in bed, there was a brilliant flash of lightning and he was surprised and alarmed to see Mister Harry Reeves standing at the other side of the road, almost directly opposite his own window, standing there in the pouring-down rain all dressed out in old clothes and a ball cap, looking wild as he could be. It frightened Sugar at first, but then he realized that Mister Harry must be drunk, and he raised the window and said: "Mister Harry, you go on in home outta this rain!"

Mister Harry had jumped about a foot off the ground and run like a rabbit.

Some Mister Harry, Sugar thought, remembering the incident. That man musta been drunk as Cootie Brown. First time I ever knew Mister Harry would get a load on like that and go wandering around in the rain. You cain't tell about these white folks, though. They sure can fool you sometimes.

Looking out across the square toward the courthouse, Sugar thought about Mister Harry and how high he had jumped, and he began to laugh. He shook silently with laughter, thinking about it. Some Mister Harry, all right. You cain't tell about these white folks, I declare you cain't.

2

When Elsie Cotter awoke she didn't feel well at all. She felt like she might be going to have another one of her headaches. It was only six o'clock, half an hour earlier than she ordinarily got up, and her father was not awake yet, so she stayed where she was in bed, trying to go back to sleep. She knew she couldn't though, and then she realized it was raining. A pleasant, cool steady rain was falling on the roof and water was running from the eaves, splashing into more water on the ground; the whole world outside her window had a watery sound, even the cars passing in the wet street. It came back to her then about the storm during the night, and she got up and raised the shade to look out.

But then she remembered about the money and the morning was spoiled for her again. A heaviness developed suddenly at the back of her eyes. She got back into bed.

Well, she thought, of all the people in the world for it to belong to, it had to be that woman. She wants the key back, does she? I wonder what she'd say if the key was all I returned. Nothing probably. Just look down her nose at me for a thief, and that would be the one thing I *couldn't* endure.

She prodded the pillow and rolled over, looking out the window. She could see the branches of the squat, dead mulberry tree that stood by the back porch, and beyond that the roof of the Jenkins' garage. There were several fist-sized rocks, a bicycle tire and a tin can on the garage roof, thrown up there by the little Jenkins boy; he was always throwing things. Mill class of people. Above the garage roof the sky was low and gray and lumpy looking. It would probably rain all day, maybe for several days. Miss Cotter yawned and stretched her heavy legs. I'd like to throw it in her face, she thought. I'd like to walk up to that fine house of hers and throw it right in her common face. She raised herself in bed to see if it was possible to see the Walker house from her bedroom window, but it wasn't. The hill on Baird Drive was in the way.

I wonder what they're doing over there now, she thought. At six o'clock they won't even be up yet. They probably get up around eight-thirty and go down and have breakfast all ready and waiting for them. For all I know, she may have breakfast in bed. She's the type. She'd do it that way to show off. Two cars and a station wagon, and just the four of them there to drive all those cars. And that daughter of hers that married the Whittaker boy, running off to Birmingham last fall to enter a dog in a dog show. Can you head that? My God, they slept with dogs three generations ago. Hound dogs. They get all that from the movies. They go to these trashy movies and try to imitate them—breakfast in bed, dog shows, colored maids, cocktails. They're a fine bunch, now aren't they? Looking down their nose at people who can trace their family practically back to the seventeenth century. Money. If you've got money you're somebody; if you don't have it you're nobody. That's how they all look at it today. It's all money now, and they've got it. Well, I've got some of it too, and I'm just half a mind to keep it, out of spite. No, I can't do a thing like that. What am I saying? My grandfather would turn over in his grave.

There was an explosion of coughing in the next room, and Elsie could hear the old man floundering around in his bed, making the springs creak with his weight. She lay very still, listening and hoping he would go back to sleep. She wasn't ready to get up yet; she had some more thinking to do. After a while he was quiet again.

She turned her pillow over to find a cool spot, and scissored her legs around to a new position in the bed. The rain drummed steadily on the roof, the water dribbled from the eaves, and now and then a damp cool draft of air would bulge the white curtains delicately She wished there was someone to bring her in a cup of coffee.

The nice thing about the old days, she thought, was that everybody knew everybody else, and the town was small and quiet and shady—a *pleasant* place to live. People played croquet. Of course it wasn't a big place now, but there was a great difference. A great difference. For instance, in those days fine old families were looked up to, whether they had money or not. Money didn't mean so much then. Look at the Proctors, what fine people they were then. And the Byjohns, and the Pontiffs. She could remember playing hopscotch under the big leafy beech trees with Jane and Zelma Pontiff, all of them wearing little white pinafores, and they must have looked like figures in a painting, under those big friendly trees. Now where were they? Jane and Zelma living all alone in that horrible old Gothic house, penniless and pathetic. Even the beech trees were gone; cut down so they could widen the street. Their father had been shot to death by old man Dave Fairchild and his half brother. There was violence in those days, too. They shot him as he came down the courthouse steps, and then when Will Pontiff was down, lying there on the ground, Dave Fairchild had got down from his horse and shot him again. It was the only stain against the Fairchild name. But even the Fairchilds were not the people they once were. Money. Too much of it.

I don't know, though, she thought. It's a blessing and a curse, I guess. You can't live right with it, and you can't live without it. It's terrible to be poor. It's humiliating, even when you know there are more important things in life. Look at us, for example. I have to quibble about groceries, I have to buy the old lettuce and that terrible cheap coffee. Me, a Morgan on my mother's side. I don't know what it's eventually coming to, either. Because I won't be able to work forever. I guess we'll end up on public welfare. Think of it. And really the worst part of it all is that nobody will even care. The old people are all gone, or else they're poor too, or have forgotten who you are. My God, we are pathetic; Papa and me. And there's nothing so bad as to be poor and humiliated and humble. Especially if you once *were* somebody. I don't care for a lot of money, I honestly don't, but I do wish I could walk in a store just once and ask for the best instead of the cheapest. I wish I could wear just one new, nice dress, and shoes that didn't look like they came from a bargain basement. Is that asking too much? I have to actually pay the bills on installments. I have to accept charity. It's the truth, I won't deny it. Papa and me, we're just pathetic old people with nowhere to turn. No family and not even friends any more, living with riffraff because it's cheap. Cheap. My God, money is everything.

She buried her face in the pillow to cry, but no tears would come. She just lay there feeling smothered. Finally she got up and crossed the room to her vanity and opened the drawer. She brushed the handkerchiefs aside and picked up the small kidney-shaped leather purse. It was Mexican made, tooled leather. She took out the fat wad of bills and transferred them to her own shabby black pocketbook and snapped it shut.

There, she said to herself. It's wrong, but I'm going to do it anyway. I'll throw that smelly little purse in the furnace and nobody will ever be the wiser. I know it's wrong, and I don't care. This afternoon I'll take the money to the bank and then maybe we'll at least be able to pay Dr. Clemmons a part of what we owe him. I'm stealing now and I'm not sorry, not even ashamed to admit it. I honestly don't care anymore. That's what it's come to.

She went back to bed again, and this time she was able to cry, a little.

3

Frank Dupree was pleased with the rain because on rainy days more people wanted a cab. He drove around the still-deserted courthouse square and pulled up at his regular stand beside the sulphur well. He was a little early, but it paid to be early; it looked like a good day to him.

After a few minutes Joe Satterfield, who drove Morgan's only other taxi, drew up beside him. Joe was a fat sloppy man, in Frank's opinion, and he couldn't see how anybody would want to ride with him. Joe had kinky hair that he brushed straight back so that his head looked a lot like a Jew. Frank suspected him of being a Jew, anyway. Joe owned a three-legged dog that hopped around town trying to follow his cab.

"Morning, Frankie," Joe said. "Looks like a good day for us, eh?"

"If it don't quit and clear up," Frank said. He was pretty sure it wouldn't, but he never liked to agree unequivocally with anything Joe said. After all, they were competitors.

Nish Calloway, who cooked for the Claytons, always went to work a little earlier than she needed to, because she rode in with her husband and he had to be at the hosiery mill at six o'clock sharp. She didn't mind though, because it gave her time to make a pot of coffee and read the morning paper before she carried it in to Mr. Clayton.

This morning when she arrived she knew there was a row on. She could hear them upstairs railing at Mister Bill. Old man Clayton was foghorning away up there.

"Don't lie to me, son," she heard Mr. Clayton shout. She hung up her coat and hat and pushed the dining-room door open so she could hear.

"All right, so I was drinking," Mister Bill said. "I'm old enough to drink if I want to, and the car happens to be mine, I paid for it myself. If I want to tear it up, I can't see where it's any concern of yours."

"You *can't*, eh?"

"Oh but son, it *is* our concern," Mrs. Clayton wailed. "You might have been killed and you're all we've got in this world."

"Mother, for God's sake. The car wasn't hurt, just a tiny scrape on one fender—you'd think I demolished it, for God's sake."

"That's not the point," the old man bellowed. "The point is what *could* have happened. You were drunk, that's what you were. And stop saying for-God's-sake."

"Look, Dad, I happen to be twenty-nine years of age, and—"

"You're *not*, Billy," Mrs. Clayton moaned. "You *know* you won't be twenty-nine till the fourteenth of August."

"All right, for God's sake! I'm only twenty-eight and eleven-twelfths, then! But I'm old enough to take a drink if I want to, and I won't be scolded like a damn child for it!"

80

"William Randolph Clayton!" Mrs. Clayton exclaimed in dismay.

Charlie Banks, the night marshal, was just going off duty when the town clock struck six. He paused at the door of the city hall, fished a big gold watch from his pocket and looked at it until he heard the mill whistle blow. Then he gave a little nod of satisfaction and went on in to leave his gun and his badge before going home to bed. He was glad of the rain, too, because it had been hard to sleep in the daytime these hot days.

Diagonally across the street, Harvey Campbell was unlocking the door of the Blue Moon Cafe.

4

At six forty-five Shelley and Helen were in the kitchen making coffee. The girls were still asleep and Jimmy had been up and fed and put back to bed again. As they waited for the coffee to perk, Shelley looked out the windows at the weather.

"Well," he said, "I guess this more or less settles it. No fishing today."

"It's too bad," Helen said. "You were all set for it, weren't you?"

"Sorta. But it's a good thing, really. The farmers needed it, and I've got the whole rest of the summer to fish in. I never thought it would happen though. Yesterday evening there wasn't a sign of a weather change anywhere."

"What about some breakfast? You want to eat now?"

"No, let's drink some coffee first and have a cigarette."

Helen got up and went out through the living room to the front door to get the paper. When she came back, Shelley was pouring two cups of coffee and the nutty roasted smell of it permeated the room. "If that's as good as it smells, it ought to be good," she said.

"The secret of good coffee is making it slow," Shelley said. "It's like making love to a woman. The longer it takes, the better."

"You Shelley."

81

"What does the paper say?"

She handed it over to him. "You read it. Same old thing. Car wrecks and Commies and the high cost of living. All I do any more is read the funnies. And they're not funny."

"That's a fact." He scanned the paper briefly and pushed it away. "Does Creta come today?"

"No, I gave her Saturdays off. You know Nigras, they hate to work on Saturday, they like to be in town."

"How's she working out anyway? I meant to ask you."

"All right. She's not as good as Sally was, of course, but we'll never find another Sally."

"No, I'm afraid not."

"She was all right. She was a good Nigra."

"Most of them nowdays try to be too familiar. They want to sit in the living room and call you by your first name."

"The trouble with most of them, they try to act like white people," Shelley said. "There's nothing wrong with being a Nigra. Looks like they'd try to act like it."

"Well, they want to get up in the world, and in a way you can't blame them. Look at how most of them have to live."

"Yeah, I guess so. I don't know. We don't treat them right, and that's a fact. Even when you try, you can't treat them right."

"Why, I wonder."

Shelley sipped his coffee and shook his head. "I don't know. We just don't think of them as our equal. We can't. It's like it was something you're born with. You can talk all you please about what you *ought* to do and how you *ought* to treat them, but back in the back of your head you just don't really believe it. There's an instinct in a white man—at least a Southern white man—to not look on a Nigra as his equal. What you think and what you feel is two different things."

"It's a shame, too," Helen said. "I try to be nice to them, but somehow it just goes against the grain to have one call me Helen instead of Miz Martin."

"Like when I went to Chattanooga for the attic fan," Shelley said. "I stopped for this light on Georgia Avenue, and the instant it changed, a car behind me began blowing the horn. That always burns me up, but when I looked in the mirror I saw it was a nigger taxicab. I swear it went all over me. I wanted to get out and raise all kinds of hell with him, just because he was a nigger. It made me twice as mad. Now, that don't make sense when you stop and think about it. A Nigra ought to have as much right as anybody to blow his horn at you. But that's how I felt. What I *thought* had nothing to do with it. You can't help how you feel."

"Yeah. And take the way all of us feel about the Jews. The Jews have always been a persecuted race. Read your Bible. There's something there that rubs us the wrong way. It may be wrong for us to feel that way, but there it is. But there's a *reason* why Jews are persecuted. They rub us the wrong way. People are always yelling about don't persecute the Jews, as if there was no reason for it—as if the trouble was all with us. There's a reason, all right. Anything that goes on as long as that has is bound to have a damn good reason behind it. Instead of them yelling at us for persecuting the Jews, I wish they'd yell at them awhile and tell them to stop rubbing everybody the wrong way."

"For me it's a lot different between Jews and Nigras," Helen said. "I *like* Nigras, I honestly do, I just don't want them in my living room calling me Helen. But I can't use those Jews at all, don't even like to be around them."

"All the same, it's a damn shame," Shelley said. "It's too bad that anybody has to get pushed around."

Helen lit a cigarette and looked at the match thoughtfully. "What about the Chinese, Shelley? Are they really all that bad?"

"There again it's owing to how you feel. The Chinaman is a colored man too, a yellow man, but I liked them myself. Of course, we couldn't leave anything laying around or they'd steal you blind, but I like a Chinaman. I'll take a Slopey anytime over say a Limey. The trouble with a Limey, is he's got no sense of humor. A Chinaman can laugh at anything. He'll even laugh at a dead man. I liked the Chinese all right, myself. I wouldn't mind to go back to China someday, if it wasn't for the Reds."

"Well, tell me this," Helen said. "Is it true what they say about Chinese women?"

They both laughed and Shelley got up and headed for the coffeepot again. "That's something I wouldn't know about, old lady. You'll have to ask somebody else on that."

"I bet. Shelley Martin, I bet you fooled around with plenty of them in your day." She was watching him closely, smiling.

"No, so help me, Helen. I never did."

"And how long was it you were over there?"

"Seventeen months."

"Listen, Mister Man, I know you better than that. You wouldn't go seventeen days, not to mention seventeen months. What makes you lie like that?"

"What makes you so nosy?"

"All right, but just don't try to kid me. I know you, Shelley Martin."

"Come on," he said, "where's that breakfast you were talking about?"

While they were eating breakfast the rain picked up again and pounded heavily on the roof; there was no wind, just the straight hard rain. "We're in for a day of it with the kids," Helen said. "I dread these kind of days when they can't go out to play. Maybe I'll get the sitter over so's I can get out for a bit in the afternoon."

"They wreck the place, don't they?"

"Well, they get bored. You know how it is. They'll sew and color and play dolls for a while, but around two or three in the afternoon they get restless and that's when the trouble begins. Even Jimmy gets bored."

"That's when you need TV."

"You said it. Shelley, why don't you go down and see about one today? There's no point in putting it off, and we'd all enjoy it so."

"I could get the series, couldn't I?"

"Come on, what do you say?"

"All right, I'll go down right after lunch and see what they've got to offer."

"What's wrong with this morning?"

"It's raining."

"Oh, pooh. I bet you'll put it off and won't go at all. Why do you always put things off?"

"Well, for one thing, I've got to go to the bank and there's no sense making two trips in the rain. I've got my check to deposit."

"Isn't the bank open this morning?"

"Yes, but it's too crowded on Saturday morning. That's when

all the farmers come in to see about their loans. Don't worry, I'll go this afternoon. I promise you."

"And will you buy one?"

"If they make me a nice deal, sure."

"You can call it my anniversary present," Helen said. "I won't ask for another thing the rest of the year."

Shelley laughed. "All right, you're going to get your TV, don't make a lot of rash statements."

"You're sweet, Shelley."

"So are you."

"No, I mean really. I'm ashamed of the way I nag you sometimes."

"Is there any more toast?"

"No, but I'll put some in."

After breakfast was over, Shelley picked up the paper and went to the bathroom. Helen began to clear up the dishes.

5

Dill and Preacher were sitting at a table and Harper was in the phone booth up near the front of the restaurant, making a long-distance call.

"What you going to have?" Dill said to Preacher.

"I don't know. A couple of eggs and ham. Maybe a side order of hotcakes."

"You're going to eat all that this morning?"

"That's right. I'm hungry."

"How can you be hungry? With a day like's ahead of us today I don't see how you can have any appetite at all."

"Why shouldn't I have any appetite?"

"Aren't you a little nervous?"

"No."

"No, I guess you're not," Dill said. "You slept like a baby last night."

"Sure I did. Anything wrong with that?"

"I bet you never even knew it rained. You didn't even hear that storm we had, did you?"

"What if I didn't? What's wrong with getting a good night's rest?"

Dill shook his head. "Nothing bothers you, does it, Preach?"

"You bother me."

"I mean the nerves. I swear I don't believe you got a nerve in your body. Me, I'll do well to get down a cup of coffee and sweet roll. You're going to order the whole goddam menu."

"I'll tell you what," Preacher said. "Suppose you order what you want and let me order what I want. Okay?"

"Wise guy."

"No, just minding my own business. It's a good habit to get into. You ought to try it sometime."

"All I said is what are you having for breakfast and he jumps down my throat."

"You annoy me," Preacher said. "You get on my nerves."

"You haven't got any nerves; how could I get on your nerves?"

"How about the underwear, did you change it this morning or not?"

"Go to hell."

Preacher gave a high soft giggle.

The waitress came over to the table then and handed each of them a menu. She put down two tumblers of water and two sets of silverware rolled tightly in paper napkins.

"There's another party with us," Dill said. "You'll want to set another place."

"Aw right," the waitress said. She was a big girl with a wart in her eyebrow. "You want to go ahead and order or what?"

"I'll order for him," Dill said. "He told me what he wants. One egg sunny-side up, bacon, toast and coffee. I'll have a cup of coffee and do you have sweet rolls?"

"No, doughnuts though."

"All right, a cup of coffee and a doughnut."

"You mean two doughnuts, don't you?"

"No, just the one."

"They come two in a package."

"Look, I don't care if they come twenty in a package. One doughnut is all I happen to want."

"*Okay*," the waitress said, giving him a hard look. "The man wants one doughnut." She turned to Preacher. "What's yours?"

"Mine's a boy, what's yours?"

"Ha, ha, very funny. Let me know whenever you get ready to order."

"I'm ready now, only I don't see it on the menu."

"If it ain't on there it ain't for sale."

Preacher looked at Dill and arched his eyebrows. "Must be for free then, eh, Dill?"

"Oh, go on and order for God sakes," Dill said disgustedly.

"All right. Everybody's a little nervous this morning. I'll have a couple of scrambled eggs with ham, toast and coffee, plus a side order of hotcakes or either hash-brown potatoes if you haven't got the cakes."

"We got the cakes."

"Cakes, then."

When the waitress left the table Dill sighed and began to fumble with his silverware. "I don't know," he said. "I still got a feeling we're going about this all wrong."

"About what all wrong?"

"Coming down here ahead of time. Hanging around and letting everybody get a look at us."

"Harper wanted to look things over good before we made our move."

"I know what Harper wanted, but I still ain't sure it was the smart thing to do."

"All right, how would you of handled it, Einstein?"

"I wouldn't have come here ahead of time like this, I'll tell you that much. I wouldn't have spent two days parading around letting everybody in town see me."

"I'm not worried."

"No, I know *you're* not worried. In order to worry you got to first have something to worry with—a brain, in other words."

"Now who's the wise guy?"

"Take that bag, for instance, that waitress. She's going to remember us for them as clear as a picture. That old coon at the hotel, he's going to describe us too. Any number of people."

"Just the same, it won't help them any. Once we make Memphis it's Katie bar the door."

"Once we make Memphis," Dill said. "Brother, don't I hope you're right though."

"You got the willies, that's all's the matter with you, Dill."

"Yep, I got the willies, all right. Like I never had them before. I've had the wrong feeling about this thing from the start. It sounds too easy somehow. Too pat. If you ask me, we better watch our step mighty careful along about three o'clock this afternoon."

"Here comes Harp. Let's see what he found out."

Harper sat down and unrolled his knife and fork; Preacher adjusted his hearing aid.

"Well, what's the deal?"

"He leaves Birmingham at ten o'clock," Harper said. "That'll put him in here around one."

"He's not coming *here*, I hope," Dill said.

"No, what I mean he'll be in position by that time. I told him we'd come out and contact him around one-thirty or two."

"In the car."

"That's right, in the car."

"I wonder," Dill said.

"You said last night you'd let me do all the worrying about the car."

"I will. I'll just be glad when it's over, that's all. Somehow, getting that car worries me more than anything."

"What about the truck?" Preacher said.

"The truck is ready, Tennessee plates and all."

"I hope that Slick don't get spooked," Dill said. "It's one thing that worries me. I got no confidence in a nigger."

"Make up your mind which it is you're going to worry about," Preacher said. "The car or the nigger."

"I'll worry about both of them till it's over," Dill said. "We're not going about this right."

"We're going about it right," Harper said. "You just try and settle down a little. Did you order for me?"

"Yeah."

"And watch what you're saying, too. We're all talking too loud."

"Dill managed to have a argument with the waitress," Preacher said.

"Aw, that's a damn lie, I didn't either. Who was it tried to pick her up?"

"You call that trying to pick somebody up? I was just kidding around."

"Whatever you were doing, knock it off," Harper said. "Both of you."

"Here comes our breakfast," Dill said.

6

Boyd Fairchild awoke suddenly, as he always did the morning after a drinking party. One moment he was deep in oblivious sleep; the next moment he was wide awake without having moved any muscle except those of his eyelids. It was as if a switch had been thrown in his head. He lay there for a minute on his side looking at the pale yellow wallpaper three feet away, and then he heard the diminishing sigh of the commode and knew what it was that had waked him. As he rolled over he saw Emily coming out of the bathroom with a glass of Alka Seltzer in one hand, a cigarette in the other. She was wearing only the top of her pajamas.

"How do you feel?"

"Like the wrath of God," she said. "How do you feel?"

"I don't know, it hasn't dawned on me yet. Is there any Dexedrine left?"

"Afraid not."

He watched her drain the glass and set it on the dresser. She stood very straight for a moment with her eyes closed, face pale. Then she sat down on the bench in front of the dresser, leaned her elbows on her knees and began to rub her eyes with the heels of her hands. "It's raining," she said.

"Is it? I guess the fishing trip's off then."

"What fishing trip?"

"Shelley and I had planned to go this afternoon."

There was a silence for a while; Emily looked around the room and groaned. "My god. Why do we do it, Boyd?"

"I don't know. I've asked myself the same thing a thousand times."

"This is the hang-over of the year, no fooling. I feel like I had a hat on about three sizes too little for me, know what I mean?"

He nodded. "Only with me it's a big lead ball inside my head. Whenever I move, it rolls back and forth."

"And sort of *thuds?*"

"That's it."

"I've got one of those too." She leaned forward again and rubbed her eyes with the heels of her hands. The cigarette, held outward between her fingers, sent up a ribbon of smoke that followed the curve of her head and spooled off into the air above her. "Boyd," she said without looking up, "we made love last night, didn't we?"

"Yes."

There was a moment of silence.

"Did you use a thing?"

He looked at her, but she wouldn't look back. She kept her face in her hands. "No, I didn't," he said.

There was a longer silence.

"Well," she said, "it was the wrong time of the month to get careless."

This angered him. "Why do you have to say careless? Why do you always look at it that way?"

She said nothing.

"What's the matter with you anyhow, Emily?"

"Nothing's the matter with me except I'm young and I'd like to stay that way a little longer."

"Is it going to make an old woman of you, just having one baby?"

"Oh, let me alone, I don't feel like fighting. Not this morning, please."

"I'm not fighting; I'm asking a simple question. I don't understand you, Emily. Sometimes I don't understand you at all."

"Neither do I."

They were silent again, hearing the rain outside which seemed to amplify the silence of the room. Boyd got up and walked carefully to the bathroom. He took a couple of aspirins, drank some water and brushed his teeth, and looked at himself in the mirror. His eyes were bloodshot and his mouth looked red and bruised. He tried to wash his face, but bending over the basin made him dizzy, so he wet a towel, wiped his face with it and let it go at that. When he went back to the bedroom Emily was sitting just as before, with her elbows on her bare knees. He looked at her and felt a little sorry for her.

"Nothing will come of it," he said. "It's not all that easy."

"I suppose not."

"Some people try for years without having a baby."

She said nothing.

"You want me to make some coffee?"

"That would be nice," she said. "We need something."

He sat down again on the edge of the bed and shook his head. "This is awful. Maybe we ought to go back to sleep awhile."

"I couldn't sleep. I've been awake since practically dawn."

"It's a sort of guilty feeling, isn't it?"

"Very. You always feel like everybody else was cold sober and you were putting on a disgusting performance of some kind."

"I don't think we were any drunker than the rest of them. Look at Wally Faulk."

"I do wish we hadn't though. No fooling, I feel *aw*ful."

"Come on back to bed," he said.

"It wouldn't help. Besides, Mother'll probably be over any minute. I've got to put up some kind of a front."

She got up and walked to the window, peering through the Venetian blind. Boyd watched her, looking at her bare thighs beneath the pajama shirt, and again he felt a desire for her. She had always been more appealing to him at times like this. He wondered why. Something about the melancholy look she had. The tangled hair and general air of dissolution. A thing like that appealed to a man at times. Like blues music, he thought, there's something about it. Something sad and earthy and don't-give-a-damn. Something low-down and at the same time beautiful.

"Don't you want to come back to bed a little while?"

She looked at him to see if he had meant what she thought. "I'm sorry, darling. I just don't think I could. I'm in bad shape, really. I'm sorry."

"All right. I just thought it was a nice day to be in bed—raining and all."

"You going to make that coffee?"

"Yes. Put your pants on though."

She smiled and came back to the bed to kiss him. "I'm sorry, darling. Don't be mad."

"I'm not. It was just a passing thought." He got up and looked at the clock. "You feel like breakfast too?"

"I doubt it. I might be able to swallow some orange juice and toast."

"I think I'll eat a raw egg."

"Don't let me see you do it, for *God* sakes."

Chapter Seven

At one-thirty that afternoon the rain had slacked off a little, but there was no sign of a change in the weather. It was going to rain on for quite awhile yet. The sky was still solid and gray with overcast, and there was no trace of wind or even a breeze, just the rain falling as warm as tears and the thirsty grass and trees drinking it up. The public square was not as busy as normal on a Saturday afternoon; the cars were fewer and they went slowly with the windshield wipers flagging; a few people hurried across at the corners carrying umbrellas or walking with their heads down and their collars turned up, and now and then a woman who had forgotten her umbrella would sprint from a parked car to the shelter of a store, holding a newspaper over her head. On the courthouse lawn the big maple trees stood silent and dripping, and the pigeons that clustered under the cornice and around the dome of the old red brick building shouldered each other fretfully for a place in the dry. The brass Civil War cannon was dull and wet, and atop the monument the old Confederate trooper looked out at the little town with water dripping from the bill of his kepi.

As it happened, Shelley failed to make the light. It was green when he turned the corner, and before he was halfway down the block it went yellow and then red, reflected on the wet pavement like a smear of bright red paint. He stopped, and when he did, a man waiting at the curb came over and tapped on the glass.

"How about a lift down the block?"

Shelley nodded and the man came around in front of the car and got in. He was a neat-looking man wearing a blue gabardine suit that was dark on the shoulders from the rain.

"I'm only going to the next corner," Shelley said.

"That'll be fine," the man said. He had unbuttoned his coat as he got in, and now suddenly there was a gun in his hand. A revolver with a long thin barrel like a target pistol. When Shelley saw it his scalp prickled.

"Turn right when the light changes," the man said. "You won't get hurt; all we want is the car. Just do like I tell you and don't get excited."

When the light went green, Shelley turned the corner and looked down at the gun again. His mouth and throat felt dry. "Mind telling me what the hell this is all about?"

The man didn't answer; he simply smiled as if that question was exactly the one he had expected. "You see those two fellows standing up there by the used-car lot?"

"Yes."

"Stop and let them get in. Do just what I say now and you'll be all right. We're not going to hurt you."

Shelley drove carefully up the block, gripping the wheel. He stopped at the car lot, and the two men got in the back seat. One was a tall man wearing glasses and a hearing aid; the other was shorter and heavily built, with an undershot jaw. He carried a cheap, imitation-leather suitcase.

"Now turn to your right again," the one with the gun said. "Head out of town like you was going to Birmingham."

Not another word was spoken until they were well out of town and going into the stretch of curving road through the river hills. As they took the second curve of the hill road, the man with the undershot jaw craned his neck around and looked out the rear window; then he settled back in his seat and let go a heavy sigh, as if he had been holding his breath for a long time.

"Nice," he said.

The man sitting beside Shelley laid the pistol across his lap and took out a pack of cigarettes. "Care for a cigarette?"

Shelley shook his head. "What is this?" he said. "Mind telling me now?"

"I already told you all I can, friend. It happens we need a car, and you drew the lucky number."

"All right, you can have the car."

One of the men in the back seat gave a high soft giggle, and Shelley felt his scalp prickle again.

Emily Fairchild was lying on the sofa with her shoes off, drinking coffee and listening to the phonograph. It was a gloomy day, partly because of the weather and partly because of her hang-over, and she had picked the *Swan Lake* album as music to fit the mood. Her gaze wandered aimlessly over the ceiling and then down the opposite wall to where the black-framed Lautrec posters hung precisely in a row. One of the pictures, her favorite, showed a man in a black hat and black cape holding a rolled paper in his left hand. The man had on a long red scarf, one end of which hung down his back. She looked at this picture for a while, then she sighed and closed her eyes.

I wonder if it did happen last night, she thought. I wonder if last night was the night.

She opened her eyes and looked up at the ceiling again.

Let's see now, she thought. It was two weeks ago last what? Last Thursday. Well, that makes it just about wrong, all right. Just about exactly wrong. Damn the luck. Damn the rotten, drunken luck. Why do we always do that when we're drinking? Why, always, must we get that way and then be careless? He did it deliberately too, I bet. No, I mustn't say that. Boyd wouldn't do a thing like that, much as he might want to. But damn it all, *why*?

Maybe it won't happen though. It's not really so easy. Look at Madge and Steve. They tried for over two years—even went to doctors about it, and then finally had two in a row. You can't tell. I guess I don't need to worry. But you can't help worrying, damn it. You can't control worrying. If only we *hadn't*. Or had waited till this morning.

Well, what's done is done, I guess. I'll just have to wait and see. Poor Boyd. I mustn't upset him about it. I made enough trouble for him last night. Maybe I could take a little quinine. He'd never know the difference. Where would I get it though? I could never fool Dr. Huff on something like that. I'll play golf. And run up the stairs.

She closed her eyes and sighed and rocked her head back and forth on the pillow.

What's the matter with me anyhow? she thought.

She tried again to listen to the music, and then after a while Boyd came in and she had to collect herself. He sat down facing her and began to file his nails.

"I was just thinking," he said, "how nice a beer would go right now. A nice, ice-cold suds with about an inch of cuff on it."

"Stop torturing me," she said.

"They have it down at the poolroom, you know."

"I know. How do they get away with that anyhow?" Maybe if we talk, she thought, I can get my mind off it.

"They get away with it the same way they get away with the whisky," Boyd said.

"But that's different. When they sell you whisky, you take it home and drink it at your own risk; but from what I hear, you can drink beer right there in the poolroom. Practically like a saloon or something."

"You take it in the john," Boyd said. "You latch the door and swill it down and throw the empty in the trash bucket. The trash bucket in there is always full of empty beer cans."

"That's what I mean. It looks like they'd be caught, being so flagrant about it."

"You know perfectly well why they don't get caught. Ace Kelley pays the Law and Order to stay the hell out; that's why they don't get caught."

"Well, I've heard that, but I don't necessarily believe it."

"You're blind then, if you don't believe it. Hobbs and all that crowd take a pay-off. They could stop this bootlegging any time they felt like it. Hell, Ace the same as told me he was paying off. Everybody knows it."

"I bet Dad doesn't know it. Darling, do you *have* to file your nails?"

"Sure he knows it." Boyd put the file down. "He just can't do anything about it, that's all. A circuit judge can't go out and arrest people; he has to depend on the officers for that. Besides, you're always going to have crooked Law as long as you have prohibition. It's been that way since time immemorial. The only sensible thing is to have legalized liquor. I'm for state-owned stores like they have in Huntsville and Birmingham, myself. That way you control it."

"I suppose so. But try telling your mother that."

"I know it. Try telling any of these older people that."

They were silent for a while.

"The whole thing goes back to religion," Boyd said. "This is the Bible Belt, and down here the devil is a bottle of liquor. It's the worst sin you can commit, according to the way they look at it."

"Why do they look at it that way I wonder?"

"Search me. Methodists and Baptists just happen to be liquor haters, that's all. At the Baptist church they don't even use real wine to take Communion."

"Will you change those records?"

Boyd got up and went over to the phonograph. "I think if I were going to join the church, I'd be an Episcopalian," he said. "They take a more liberal attitude toward drinking and things like that."

"I could never join that church," Emily said. "I had a roommate at Stevens that was an Episcopalian, and I used to go to church with her once in a while. No thanks. All that kneeling and chanting. They're nothing but watered-down Catholics."

"Not quite. They don't go in for all this dogma the way the Catholics do. Bodily ascensions and all that nonsense."

"They have a good bit of it though. And that creed, or whatever it is they say, it lays it right on the line about believing in the Holy Catholic Church. I know. I used to go with this roommate of mine."

"Still I think it beats what you have to put up with down here at the Baptist. No fooling, half the Baptist preachers in this part of the country aren't even literate, for God's sake. Old Shallowford says *irregardless*, and *sang* for *sing*. 'The congregation will please stand and sang hymn number so-and-so.' At least the Episcopal ministers are educated. The Catholics too."

"Well have it your way. But I still say I could never join that church. Catholics. Devout Catholic. Did you ever notice that Catholics are always referred to as 'devout Catholics'? 'He was a devout Catholic; she was a devout Catholic.' The two words go together like they were hyphenated. Aren't there any 'devout' Presbyterians, or 'devout' Moslems?"

"How did we get off on this anyway?"

"Talking about beer and prohibition and the high cost of bootleg whiskey. And that reminds me," she said, "I've got to go to the bank this afternoon. Mother gave me a little check. Will you run me down?"

"Yes, but let's wait awhile and see if the rain won't let up. It's still raining out there."

He got up and left the room, and Emily gazed up at the ceiling again. Poor Boyd, she thought. Poor baby. He's trying to cheer me up.

3

When they left the hills the road straightened out again on a gentle downgrade past cotton fields and woodlands, and the rain was still falling, spattering against the windshield where it was cut cleanly and quickly away by the wipers. Shelley could make no sense out of what was happening to him; he felt stunned. I'm in trouble, he thought. I'm in a hell of a jam of some kind. But what?

The men were silent, and there was a tenseness about all of them. In the car there was a charged, electric quietness. They've killed somebody or robbed a store, Shelley thought. But when he looked back on it in his mind, there had been no excitement in the town as they went through. the men had gotten into the car without any particular hurry. There was a tenseness but no sign of hurry or fear. In fact, they had made him drive slowly, not at all like they were escaping from something. I can't figure it, he thought. But I'm in a mess all right. These boys are up to something unpleasant, and I'm right in the middle of it. What the hell *is* this anyway? He felt a vein throbbing in the side of his neck.

When they were about eight miles from town, passing through the second range of scrubby hills that faced the river, the man with the gun told him to slow down. "As soon as we come out on the straight again, you'll see a dirt road that turns off to the right," he said. "Take that road and I'll tell you when to stop."

Shelley did as he was told. It was a wide smooth chert road, a farm-to-market road, and when they had gone about a mile, the man with the gun told him to stop the car. It was not possible to see the highway from where they stopped.

97

"Now you get out and get in the back seat with the boys," the man said. "I'll drive the rest of the way."

"Oughtn't we to blindfold him?" said the man with the undershot jaw.

"Yeah, tie a handkerchief over him," said the man in front. "We won't want him to see anything from here on in."

Shelley sat between the two men in the back seat and the one who wore the hearing aid tied a handkerchief around his head, drawing the knot very tight. "Don't try to pull it off, either," he said. Shelley noticed that he had been eating onions. "If you pull it off you might see something we can't afford for you to see, and then, we might have to be a little rough on you."

"Don't worry," Shelley said. He had no intention of pulling the blindfold off.

The car started again and they drove on for another half mile or so, not talking. When they stopped the second time Shelley heard a car door slam and heard someone coming toward them across the chert road.

"Well, you finally made it," a new voice said outside the window.

"Now, watch what you say," the man in front cautioned him. "This fellow don't need to know anything, see? No names, no nothing."

"How did it go?" the strange voice asked.

"It went fine. Not a hitch anywhere, so far." They were all getting out of the car now, and Shelley felt a hand take his arm and he got out too. They were standing at the side of the road, and there was a barn nearby. He could smell it.

"Come over here a minute," said the man who had done most of the talking. "One of you stay with him, and if you hear a car or anything coming, make him get back in the car before they see him with a blindfold on."

"Why not take him on to the barn?"

"All right. I guess that would be better. Take him on to the barn, the two of you. Slick and me'll be up there as soon as we go over a couple of things."

"I thought you said no names."

"That slipped. But it don't matter. All he knows is there's a guy here called Slick. Take him on to the barn."

Shelley let them lead him away from the road and up a

sloping muddy path. It was still raining, but it was a light rain now and the men seemed to pay it no attention at all. Shelley was made to stop while they opened a gate. He heard a chain clank, and heard the soft scudding sound the corner made as they dragged the gate open. A cattle gate, he thought. He tried to place the barn in his memory, but he couldn't. There were too many farms and barns along this road to remember any of them in particular. He knew the territory though, because he had hunted it. He knew pretty well where he was.

They led him up the barn lot and into the aisle of the barn. He could smell it very strongly now, the dank warm odor of straw and manure and harness leather. The ground underfoot was cushiony, and overhead he could hear the rain falling on the tin roof.

"What about taking him up in the loft?" one of the men said.

"I don't know," said the other. "We better wait and see what—what *he* says."

"I think the loft is the place for him. Up there he's really on ice, and no one sees him from the road."

"Let's wait and see."

They stood in the hall of the barn and waited, listening to the rain, and after a while Shelley heard a car door slam again (it sounded more like a truck door, he thought), and then the other two men came into the barn.

"We thought about putting him up in the loft," one of the men said. "We thought that would be a good place to hide him."

"It would be all right. It don't matter too much though, because Slick here is going to stay with him till we get back. We ought to keep an eye on him that long, at least."

"I agree," someone said. "If he was to get loose too soon he could gum the works."

"Show him how to get up the ladder."

Shelley felt himself led to the wall of the barn, and then his hands were taken and placed on the rungs of the ladder.

"Up you go," said the new voice.

"What about the rope?" someone asked.

"Right here."

"Tie him good, hand and foot. And leave the bandage on his eyes."

In the barn loft Shelley was made to lie down in the loose

hay, and he was not sure whether two or three of the men had followed him up there. They tied him securely with his hands behind his back, and then went down again. He was afraid to move, because he knew he was lying very close to the edge of the loft. He could feel an emptiness in the air in front of his face.

The men left the barn briefly; then he heard the car start—his own car—and the sound of the tires on the gravel as they turned it around. After a moment he heard a man come in the barn and climb the ladder.

"Well, how's the boy?" the new voice said. Shelley thought it sounded like a Negro.

"Listen to this," the man said, and Shelley heard a shotgun being loaded. He heard the shells go into the magazine and the *clack-clack* as one was pumped into the chamber. "That's double aught buckshot," the man said. "But you'll be all right as long as you don't try any fancy routines on me."

"What do you plan to do with me?" Shelley said.

"Nothing. Just leave you here, nice and safe and dry. Somebody will find you late this evening or tomorrow morning."

There was a long silence; then Shelley heard the scrape of a match and smelled a cigarette being lighted.

"Don't you know it's dangerous to smoke in a barn?"

"I like to live dangerously."

He's a nigger all right, Shelley thought. A smart Yankee nigger. He's a mean son of a bitch, too.

"I'd give you a cigarette, only I'm not supposed to untie you," the Negro said. "But anyway you wouldn't smoke, would you? It's too dangerous in a barn." He gave a short laugh, and Shelley knew he was nervous. He's bluffing, he thought. He's talking tough for his own benefit. If I had a chance I could work on that baby. I'd make him wish he was back picking cotton.

"What are you people up to?" he asked the Negro. "It won't hurt to tell me now, will it?"

"I guess not. By the time you get back to town it'll be a week old in the papers."

"All right, what is it then?"

"We're robbing the bank."

Shelley felt something drop inside him, sickeningly. Less

100

than an hour ago he had given his pay check to Helen to deposit. She was going down with Sue Harper, while he priced a television set.

4

Sitting at his desk in the bank, Harry Reeves could not actually see the front of the hotel, because the corner Esso station was in the way, but he could see the intersection in front of the hotel; and when Miss Benson crossed on a green light—running a little to beat a car and holding her umbrella in front—he spotted her at once. Looking through the big plate-glass window, he felt his pulse give a mighty thump and a warmness suffused his groin. Miss Benson was wearing slacks. Green satin slacks that fitted her very snugly about the hips. Harry had never had the luxury of seeing Miss Benson in slacks before. This would be a real novelty. He had seen her in starched uniforms and print dresses; he had seen her in her underclothes and stark, tingling naked. But he had never before seen her in slacks. This promised a fresh delight.

He pretended to jot a memo on the pad in front of him, but actually he was waiting to see which way she would turn at the corner. If she went left it was almost certain that she was headed for the drugstore; if she went to the right it could mean anything from the beauty parlor to an afternoon movie. He hoped fervently that she would turn left, because if she went to the drugstore he could follow and get a good close look. I'm insane, he thought. But I don't care, I'm lost anyway. Please let her turn to the left.

At the corner, Miss Benson hesitated briefly and turned to the left. Harry Reeves leaped up from his desk and grabbed his hat so suddenly that Ted Proctor looked around from his window to see what was the matter.

"Got a headache, Ted," Reeves said excitedly. "I'm going to run over to the drugstore for some aspirin."

"I think there's some aspirin in the bathroom, Mr. Reeves."

"I need some fresh air anyway," Reeves said, hurrying around the little fence and out toward the door. He had forgotten his umbrella, but it was too late now. He walked quickly to the corner and crossed the street without even looking up at the light. A car skidded to a stop and the driver honked at him angrily. Reeves paid no attention. I belong in an institution somewhere, he told himself. He caught sight of Miss Benson again just as she disappeared into the drugstore.

Controlling himself, he walked past the drugstore a few paces, then stopped and snapped his fingers, as if he had just remembered what it was he had to do. This was for whatever eyes happened to be looking. Then he went into the drugstore, and without so much as a glance in Miss Benson's direction, he ordered a Coke and leaned against the fountain. Not until the Coke was placed in front of him on the marble counter did he allow himself to turn very casually, and look.

Miss Benson was seated at one of the little wire-leg tables a few steps away, thumbing through a magazine as she drank her Coke and ate her package of Nabs. She was sitting at an angle to Reeves, almost with her back to him, and that was even better luck than he had hoped for. He could look at her now without her knowing. He took one last cautious glance around the drugstore, saw Mr. Huff staring absently toward the street, and then he turned and fed his eyes. Miss Benson's ample buttocks were spread and flattened against the chair seat, and the thin material of her slacks was drawn so tight across them he could see the ridge of her step-ins where they curved across her hips into the pleasant declivity of her lap. It made him weak. He dragged his eyes away and swallowed a sip of Coke. God help me, he moaned silently. I ought to kill myself for what I'm doing now, for what I'm thinking now.

With trembling weak fingers he pulled his watch from his pocket and read the time. Eight minutes till three. In eight minutes the bank closed; he *had* to go back. No, he thought, I'll stay till the last minute. I'll take five minutes more. God help me.

He sipped his Coke, checked the drugstore again to make sure no one was watching, and then turned and fed his eyes. . . .

5

Shelley lay tied and blindfolded in the rough hay and thought: there's nothing I can do. There's not a chance in the world.

102

He was lying on his side and the loose hay scratched his face when he moved. The cotton rope cut into his wrists where they were lashed behind him, making his hands numb, and his shoulders were beginning to ache a little from the position in which his arms were drawn back. For fifteen or twenty minutes now he had been lying there, listening to the rain and thinking.

Helen will probably be out of the bank and gone by the time it happens, he thought. And even if she did happen to be there, I doubt if there'll be any trouble. No one will buck them, surely. I wonder what time it is. If I could somehow get loose, I wonder if I could get to a phone in time. Probably not. I ought to at least try though. What can I do? I'll never get loose, and if I tried, that nigger would shoot me. If I was smart I'd sit tight and hope for the best. No, I ought to at least try. A man ought to do what he can. If something happened and Helen got hurt, I'd never forgive myself. I've got to make some kind of a try at it, at least. Hell, I don't even have a pocketknife. What do I think *I* can do?

The Negro had gone down from the loft some time ago, but Shelley didn't know where. He might be outside in the truck, or he might be standing below in the hall of the barn. Very likely he was still in the barn somewhere, because the white men had told him to stay there.

Shelley wondered about this for a while, then decided to take a chance on it. He rolled carefully over on his stomach and began trying to loosen the blindfold by rubbing his face against the hay. The hay scratched him, but he made a little progress at it. He rubbed his face and the side of his head against the floor, like a cat rubbing his ears in the grass. Now and then he would stop and listen for the Negro, but there was no sound except the rain falling on the tin roof. One thing worried Shelley more than the noise he was making: he knew the planking of the loft floor had wide cracks in it, and as he rubbed his face against it he was bound to cause some of the loose hay and dust to sift through the cracks. If the Negro saw that, he'd know something was up. But it was a chance you had to take.

Before long he had worked the blindfold down over one ear and the bridge of his nose to where he could see over it with his right eye; and then finally it loosened and slid off his face, hanging around his neck. Now he could see everything.

It was a big barn, and as he had suspected, he was lying dangerously close to the edge of the loft. He squirmed back a little and looked the situation over. There were a dozen or more bales of green alfalfa hay and a lot of loose hay in the loft, and that was all. He had hoped for a pitchfork or an ax or something else that might be used as a weapon, but there was nothing but the hay. A singletree was hanging on a nail down near the foot of the ladder, but it was far out of reach. I couldn't use it on him anyway, he thought. How can you hit a man with your hands tied behind you? I haven't accomplished a damn thing. I wonder what time it is.

Looking over the edge of the loft into the aisle of the barn, he could not see the Negro anywhere. Where is that bastard? he wondered. He must be out there in that truck or car or whatever it is they have out there.

Shelley got himself into a sitting position and began inching his way toward the south wall of the barn. He was able to make some progress by stretching his legs out and scooting himself backward. When he reached the wall of the barn, he pressed his eye to a crack and looked out. He saw the wet red clay of the barnyard and nothing else. He worked his way along the wall until he found another, larger crack, and looked out again. This time he saw the truck. It was parked at the edge of the road just beyond the barbed-wire fence and about forty yards away. It was a closed delivery truck with the words *Tate Florist* scrawled fancily across it in gold letters.

How do you like that? Shelley thought. They're coming out here in my car, ditch it and then probably go right back through town in the truck. Pretty shrewd. They leave town in a green Ford headed south, and ten minutes later they're hid in the back of a florist truck with a nigger driver, headed west. Pretty clever, I must say. Goddam bastards.

He saw a puff of cigarette smoke come out of the truck window and drift away, dissolving in the rain. That's where the nigger is, he thought. He's out there in the cab of the truck, waiting. That's a break for me. Maybe I can pick these knots loose on a nail. I could go out the back of the barn and he'd never even see me.

Shelley hitched his way along the barn wall looking for a nailhead that was sticking out, but he couldn't find one. It was a well-made barn, every nail driven up. This ain't my day, he told himself. He made his way back to the edge of the loft and, being very careful, turned over on his side and began trying to saw the ropes against the plank edges. It seemed hopeless, but he had to try.

He sawed at the ropes, but it was awkward, painful work and he was in constant danger of losing his balance and falling over the edge. Not only that, it was getting him nowhere. Then as he was staring hopelessly at the green bales of hay, it dawned on him what he could do, and he got busy. Working with his feet, from a sitting position, he managed to push two bales of hay up to the edge of the loft directly above the ladder. Now, he thought. Those babies will weigh probably eighty or ninety pounds apiece. I just hope I don't miss. Because if I do I'm a goner. That nigger will shoot me as sure as hell. I've got to chance it though, and I've got to hurry. I don't see how I can miss him.

He got himself into position then, bracing his back and planting the soles of his feet squarely against the nearest bale, and then he threw his head back and yelled as loud as he could. "Help! Help!" Then he listened. He heard the door of the truck open and slam shut and the Negro running for the barn. He heard the man come in and run across the soft earth floor of the barn, and when he knew he must be reaching for the ladder, he pushed the bales over quickly, one behind the other.

There was a split second of silence, and then the bales hit and Shelley knew he hadn't missed. He heard the Negro thrashing around down there, making no outcry at all, just a choking sound.

Shelley waited a long time, sweating in the silence, getting hold of himself. Then he got ready to ease himself over the edge for the long drop to the ground.

6

About the time Reeves was leaving the bank, Boyd and Emily Fairchild were arriving. Boyd found a parking place in front of the bank, and Emily got out to go in. He stayed in the car, thinking vagrantly of this and that, and watching the people pass. He saw Miss Elsie Cotter go by and he nodded to her, but she didn't see him because of the rain on the glass. She went into the bank and Boyd wondered whether she was putting money in or taking it out. Probably putting it in, he thought. I imagine Miss Elsie has a hard time making ends meet these days. I imagine every cent she can scrape goes in the bank all right.

In the car next to his, two men were sitting. They were strangers and he wondered idly who they were. The one who sat behind the wheel kept glancing at his watch.

I need a beer, Boyd thought. I wonder if I'd have time to run over to the poolroom before Emily gets back. He lit a cigarette and let the window down a little so the smoke could get out. Now and then a raindrop would hit the edge of the glass and send a tiny spray against his neck. It was hot in the car with the windows up.

For no reason at all he began to think of the party last night, and it made him blue and remorseful again. The fuss he and Emily had on the back porch, that was bad. I wish I hadn't accused her of that, he thought. I was drunk or I never would have said that. All day we've been pussyfooting around, trying not to mention it. And then this morning, that came very near being a scene too. I feel bad. I'm hanging, brother, hanging. I need a beer. He began to hum a tune they had sung at the party last night. "Rock-a my soul in the bosom of Abraham, Rock-a my soul in the—boo-zoom of Abraham . . ." He drummed on the steering wheel with his fingers, letting his ring click against it on every other beat. May horse, he thought. What was that joke Dink told about a May horse? What is a May horse anyhow? Oh yes. A May horse will always lie down in water. What makes me think of a fool thing like that?

He saw the two men in the next car get out and walk to the door of the bank where they were met by a third man who had just come up. Shelley Martin's wife and another woman stepped out of the bank just as the men were about to go in, and one of them, a man with a face like a shark, held the door open politely.

Boyd watched Helen Martin as she got in the car with her friend. Old Shelley, he thought. I bet he enjoys that. She's got a figure, that girl has. Not what you'd call pretty, but stacked up. I wonder if they ever have any trouble the way we do. Shelley has three kids, so I guess not. I envy that guy in a way. I actually do. I guess he thought I was a fool about those dye runs. Well, I don't care. I don't give a happy damn, and that's a fact. I feel rotten. R-o-t-t-e-n. I've got to have a beer before I collapse. How does Emily do it? She's feeling all right again already. Women are tougher than men, let's face it. Maybe by tonight I'll feel all right. But I need a beer. A nice, ice-cold suds. Damn these Baptists. I think I'll run on down there. She'll wait in the car.

He got out, pulled up the collar of his raincoat and started for the poolroom. Midway of the block he met the old Negro called Sugarfoot. Sugar had a paper sack under his arm.

"Look out there, Sugar."

"Hello, Mister Boyd."

"What's in the sack?"

"Pair of shoes a fellow give me. Two-tone jobs!"

"Atta boy, Sugar."

Sugar did a little step and went on down the street, laughing and shaking his head. He had taken on a few, you could tell.

In the poolroom Boyd asked for a beer and Handy James, Kelley's sidekick, gave it to him under the counter. Handy James was said to have epilepsy. Boyd laid out a half dollar and stood for a minute watching the games in progress on the smooth green tables. The colored balls rolled back and forth clicking against each other with a sound like teeth clicking together, and the players moved around the tables at the edge of the smoke-moted cones of light. Then he went into the rest room and latched the door behind him. It was a filthy, smelly place, with no window at all and only a single naked bulb hanging from the ceiling. There were a number of inexpertly drawn pictures of naked women on the walls. Boyd read one of the penciled limericks. "Here's to the girl that waits on the table . . ." He began to drink the beer quickly, tilting the can up and letting the cold beer run full into his mouth from the wedge-shaped hole in the top.

He heard the gunfire just as he was finishing his can. It was a hollow, booming sound—loud and incongruous, because there could be no doubt about what it was.

In the middle of town in the middle of the day, someone was firing a gun.

He flung the can into a corner and snatched the door open almost in a single gesture. The poolroom was frozen. The players stood in various attitudes of arrested motion, like figures in a wax museum. Even the cigarette smoke, lying in pale ribbons on the stale air, seemed to hang transfixed. Then someone shouted "That came from the bank!" and they all started for the door. Boyd pushed out into the street with the first of them and immediately saw other people running—the rainy street suddenly filled with running people. Somewhere a car horn was blowing long and loud and agonizingly, like a cry for help, and the pigeons had flushed from the courthouse dome, like scraps of paper scattered wildly against the sky.

A crowd had already gathered, babbling and shouting at the front of the bank when Boyd got there. He shoved his way through and saw Harry Reeves lying in the doorway, half in and half out, with the heavy door closed across him and his watch hanging down from his vest pocket, still turning on its gold chain. There was broken glass and blood everywhere; blood was streaked waist-high along the wet wall of the bank, as if bloody fingers had clutched at it, and in the glass of the door there were two large fuzzy-looking holes with cobwebs of cracks around them. A fresh white splinter stuck out from the frame of the door.

Boyd was the first to enter the bank—no one else seemed able to think beyond the man lying there in the rain. It was dark and gloomy inside, and there was a smell of exploded powder still in the air. Emily was the only person he saw, and the instant he saw her he knew he was much too late. She looked dead already. She was sitting in the center of the tile floor. Sitting there like a child, very erect, with her legs straight out and her head turned oddly to the side; one of her shoes had come off and was lying in front of her on the floor. There was a great dark egg-shaped blot of blood coming through the back of her yellow raincoat, and by the mild look in her face, he knew he was much too late.

Chapter Eight

If I break a leg now I'm a goner, Shelley thought. Those babies will blow me up when they see what I've done to their nigger. He was working his way carefully around the edge of the loft to a place where he could drop down to the barn floor. The Negro was lying at the foot of the ladder, beside the two bales Shelley had pushed off on him. Shelley was afraid he might land on the Negro or hit one of the bales, if he jumped from the top of the ladder, so he was edging around to the other side. I've got to try to land on my feet, he told himself, and when I hit I've got to roll with it. If I break a leg I'm out of luck. They'll shoot me just as sure as the world. The one with that thing in his ear; he'd blow my brains out for me just on general principles. I don't like the looks of that baby. I don't like any of them's looks. When they see this nigger I better be gone from here. What I can do, though, is cut the truck tires. I guess I'm too late for anything else. I don't know. If I could get to a phone it might not be too late. Now then. This is about right. It's a long way down, Jesus! But that ground is soft and I'll try to roll with it when I hit. Here goes.

He swung his legs over the edge and in one motion shoved with his hands and arched his back. He dropped clear and clean, and hit the cushiony dirt with his knees flexed. It was a fifteen-foot drop, and it jarred him in every bone and joint. He had forgotten to close his mouth, and when he hit, his teeth snapped together so hard he thought he had broken them off. He pitched forward and slightly to the side so that his shoulder dug into the manure and dirt, and then his cheek and his ear scraped, and his ear felt like it had been ripped off. He lay there for a minute numb and tingling, but he knew he was all right. He hadn't broken anything, at least. The feeling came gradually back into his feet, and his ankles began to burn; they were lashed together tightly and when he struck the ground they had bruised against each other. But what bothered him most at the moment was his ear. It felt like it was gone, scraped clean off the side of his head, and he had a sudden, violent urge to raise his hand and feel it to see if it was still there. But he couldn't reach it with his hands tied, so he arched his neck and shook his head and then rubbed the ear against the ground again. It was still there all right. It began to burn and tingle and ring, so he forgot about it and began testing his teeth with his tongue to see if they were chipped. What really mattered, though, were the legs. As soon as the feeling returned to them he sat up and began the hitching-sitting movement, edging across the barn floor to where the Negro was lying. He lost his balance once and toppled over the side of his face, but he struggled up into a sitting position again and kept going. His ear was ringing and his ankles burned, as if they were completely raw.

I wonder if he's dead, he thought, looking at the Negro. Jesus, I hope not, but I had to do it. For all I know, they're in that bank right now and Helen in there too. No telling what could happen. I had to do it.

Looking at the Negro he felt a little sick at his stomach. The man was wearing green whipcord coveralls with *Tate's Florist* stitched in longhand across the back, and under the coveralls he had on a clean white shirt and a black leather bow tie. The tie had come loose at one edge of the collar, and it was clinging to the other edge like a big butterfly. His cap, which had a white visor and matched his coveralls, was lying partly under one of the bales, squashed and twisted with just the bill and one edge of the crown sticking out. Shelley could not see the Negro's face. He hitched himself around and looked. The Negro had smooth caramel-colored skin and a very narrow mustache, hardly more than a black line, across his upper lip. His eyes were closed and his nose was bleeding, and there was a long clear string of saliva hanging from his mouth. He looked awful and Shelley felt weak and sick, looking at him. I've killed him, he thought. Just as sure as the world I've killed that man. But I had to do it. It was all I could do. No, wait a minute, he's not dead. He's sweating. Look at the sweat on him, that man's not dead. Not yet, he's not. He's in bad shape though; I imagine his neck is broken. That was a hell of a load and it must have caught him square on the head. What about that shoulder? That shoulder is broken too, it's bound to be. He couldn't lie that way. One of them must have caught his shoulder. Well, I'm sorry, but what else could I do? I had no choice about it, and he asked for it, didn't he? He would have done the same for me. He's a crook isn't he? He's an outlaw. Well, it's done anyway, whether I like it or not, and I've got to get busy now in a hurry. I haven't got long; in fact, I'm probably too late already. But I can cut the tires and at least throw a stop in them. Why the hell did this have to happen to me?

He hitched himself around to the Negro's right side again,

turned his back and with his hands behind him felt over the man's pockets for the knife. He knew there had to be a knife, because the Negro had used a knife to cut the ropes when they tied him up. He felt over the Negro's pockets and it made him sick to touch the warm flesh of the man's thigh under his clothes. The knife was there all right. It was in his pocket with half a dozen more shotgun shells. There was some money in the pocket too, and a book of paper matches. Shelley took hold of the edge of the pocket and ripped it open, feeling the shells and the money spill out on the ground behind him. He groped around until his hand touched the knife, and the, perspiring and grunting, he set to work getting the blade open. It was ticklish work, because he couldn't see what he was doing, and once he dropped the knife and had to feel around for it again. But finally he got his thumbnail under the blade and got it open, and then, holding it backward with the back of the blade up against the heel of his right hand, he began sawing at the ropes. He knew it would take a long time, because in that position he couldn't exert any force against the blade. He just had to saw, lightly, and hope the blade was sharp enough to slice through under its own weight.

He worked and sweated with his tongue in the corner of his mouth. Now and then the Negro would moan and his hands would twitch, but Shelley knew he had nothing to worry about from him. He's in bad shape, Shelley thought. I imagine I've killed me a man today. But I had no choice about it. God Amighty, I wish I'd stayed at home today. I wish I'd never heard of a goddam TV set.

Overhead the rain drummed steadily on the tin roof.

2

It was a long time before the first ambulance arrived, and when it did, there were two more right behind it. Even the Negro ambulance came, through some mistake. Both Reeves and Emily had been rushed to the hospital in private cars, and since they were the only two wounded, there was no one for the ambulances to pick up. They wailed around the square in confusion, followed by so many cars that finally there was a bad traffic jam, and people were running everywhere in the rainy streets trying to find out what had happened. The town was full of excitement. Those who had arrived early on the scene knew what had happened, and a horde of them had followed the victims to the hospital. Now they were milling around on the hospital porch and trampling the shrubbery in the yard, jabbering and calling to each other as they waited for word from the emergency room. More people hurried down the street toward the hospital, many of them running. Shopgirls, barbers, grocerymen, butchers, mechanics, men, women, children and dogs. Sid Rayburn and two men from the poolroom had brought Reeves to the hospital, and Sid's car was parked in front of the hospital now with the rear door still hanging open. There was a cluster of people around it, looking in at the blood. One woman held a little boy up to the window so he could see too. Emily had been taken in at the side door, and no one knew exactly who it was that brought her, whether it was Boyd in his own car, or some other car. It was a terrible thing, they all agreed and several people wanted to know where the hell the Law was. Tom Ed Harris, the circuit clerk, explained it for them.

"A call came in to the sheriff's office about fifteen minutes ago about a car wreck out on eleven. They said the police was needed and natually they went. I don't know if it was so, or if it was some scheme to get them out of town while this was happening. They're not back yet."

"What about the town officers?" someone asked.

"They both went with the sheriff."

"Ain't *that* a hell of a note."

"Did anybody see which way the bandits went?"

"They went out highway thirty-two, toward Birmingham," someone said. "They were driving a green fifty-three Ford."

"Didn't anybody follow them?"

"Luke Sawyer's boy did, but he turned back when they taken a shot at him. He had two girls in the car."

"Somebody ought to at least followed them."

"Listen. *You* follow them. I ain't mad at life."

"How much did they get?" someone else asked.

"Around a half million was what I heard. They took it all."

Another man spoke up. "Aw, you're out of your mind;

there's wasn't no half a million dollars in that bank, cash."

"I wonder if they got my money," said a little man wearing overalls. "My money was in that bank."

"Don't get excited, all the money's insured. You start that kind of talk and you'll cause a run on the bank."

"I still say somebody ought to made a try at following them."

Everyone was talking at once.

"Boy, won't old Hobbs' face be red about this? Him out of town when the bank is robbed."

"Something worse than his face will be red. Elections come up in September, don't forget."

"Brother!"

"We ought to kick him out of office right now," said a bald-headed man. "Those fellows made a clean getaway. He better start checking up on these calls that come in about a wreck on the highway."

"Well, boys, let's not be hasty in our judgment," Tom Ed Harris said. "Give a man a chance. He's doing an honest job."

"Honest, hell."

"What I can't see is why somebody didn't follow them to see which way they went."

"I told you they went down thirty-two."

Several more joined the group.

"Was Reeves dead when they brought him in?"

"We don't know; that's what we're trying to find out."

"How about the Fairchild girl?"

"That's something else we don't know. She was sitting up in the car when they brought her in though."

"No, she wasn't exactly sitting up, Joe. Her husband was holding her up. That was her husband that carried her in."

"Whose car was it?"

"That I don't know."

"I believe that fellow Reeves is dead, myself. Did you see him?"

"We had us a good sheriff once. Dan Birdsong. We ought to kept him."

"Hobbs is all right. He does the best he can."

"Trouble is, his best ain't near good enough. Why don't he check on those calls before he runs off up the road and leaves the town unprotected."

"Jesus Christ man, he can't check all the calls that come in that office."

"Dan Birdsong is a nitwit."

"How many times did they shoot old Reeves?"

"Nobody seems to know, but I saw three holes in the door."

"All those didn't hit him though. I heard somebody say two bullets hit a car out front."

"That don't mean anything. A bullet can go right on through a man and still hit a car."

"All I know is he was shot enough to bleed like a stuck hog."

"Whose car did they hit?"

"The bullets? Old man George Hall's, I think it was. Anyhow it was a black Buick."

"What year?"

"Christ man, I never paid any attention to what year."

"How come them to start shooting in the first place? Was Reeves trying to run or something?"

"No, the way we heard it, he was trying to get in."

"That's funny. What on earth for?"

"Search me, fellow. I wasn't there."

"And glad you wasn't, I guess."

"Who all else was in there?"

"Miss Cotter was in there. I think she and the Fairchild girl was the only ones, outside of the regular employees. She didn't get hurt though."

"Bill Cheek's wife musta been in there. She works at the bank."

"Yeah, and Jake Pratt too. I'm kin to Jake."

"I understand they locked them all in the vault when they left."

"That's what they say."

"Who got them out?"

"Tom Huff. They talked to him on the phone and told him how to get it open. There's a phone in the vault, did you know that?"

"Wasn't there no alarm or nothing they could ring when they seen it was a holdup?"

"I reckon not."

"You know, in some banks they have a button on the floor that all they have to do is step on."

114

"If somebody had followed them, we'd have had more a chance to catch them."

"I guess *you'd* of followed, and them shooting out the back window at you."

"I'd of done *some*thing."

"It's a pity you wasn't there then."

"What I don't understand is why they shot the girl."

"It beats the devil, don't it—something like this happening here?"

"I bet the Birmingham papers will eat it up."

"Well, I'm going to have to get in out of this rain, or I'll be dead myself by morning."

"Have they found out anything yet? Is Reeves dead?"

"We don't know nothing, mister. Your guess is as good as ours."

"Any you guys seen Shelley Martin?"

"Not me, Why?"

"His wife's trying to locate him."

"I heard some woman say they was going to operate on the girl. She can't be moved till they do."

"Lord, look at the mob down here, would you? Looks like the Fourth a July picnic."

"Yeah, rain and all."

"It looks to me like those people would have smothered."

"What people?"

"In the bank. The ones they put in the safe."

"They never put them in the *safe*, you dope. They put them in the vault. They's a big difference."

"It's a good thing they had that phone in there. With Reeves dead, they might never have got out."

"Nobody said Reeves was dead."

"There's how your rumors get started."

"How much did they get?"

"I heard it was a half a million."

"Boy, you like that figure, don't you? I told you while ago there ain't no half million in a bank that size."

"Listen, they ain't *nothing* in there now. From what I heard they took it all. I mean, *cleaned* it."

"You can hear anything."

"Which way did they go?"

"Somebody said down thirty-two."

"I'm the one said it. I saw them pull out."

"Why didn't you follow them?"

"Why don't a frog suck eggs?"

"I heard three people was killed."

"Well, you heard wrong."

"That woman over there ought to get her baby in out of this rain."

"Every doctor in town's in there operating, they say."

"Two or three must be cutting on the same one, then."

"Somebody said Harry Reeves just died."

"Somebody's crazy as hell. I helped carry him in. Here. See this blood on my shirt?"

"Is Harry Reeves dead?"

"No, Harry Reeves is not dead. See this? I helped carry him in. Who starts these rumors?"

"It came from the porch."

"How much did they get?"

"Which way did they go?"

"Why did they shoot the girl?"

"Wait a minute," said the man in overalls. "Is that the sheriff coming?"

"Where?"

"I thought I heard a sireen."

"It's about time."

"What in hell happened in there anyway?"

3

"It's hard to remember exactly what *did* happen," Ted Proctor said. "What I mean, it happened so fast and all. You know how it is in a case like that. You get stunned."

He was sitting in the recorder's office at the city hall, surrounded by half a dozen town councilmen who had assembled there to start an immediate inquiry. Morris Walker, council chairman, had promised an "immediate inquiry" from the courthouse steps, almost before the echo of the guns had died away, and now they were hearing what Ted Proctor had to

116

say about it. The sheriff still hadn't arrived, and four cars had been dispatched by four different councilmen to find him.

"It was five minutes till three when they came in," Ted said. "I remember because I had gone back to the vault for something and when I came out I looked up at the clock to see if it was time to close the safe yet. Mr. Reeves usually does that, but he was gone out to the drugstore, and whenever he's out, that job more or less falls to me. Well, just as I was walking back to my window, I saw these three men come in, and one of them turned around and threw the lock on the door and pulled down the blind. For a minute I couldn't hardly believe my eyes. I knew it was a robbery though. Even before they drew their guns I knew it had to be a robbery, just by that fellow drawing down the blind.

"Well, so then it happened. It seemed like everybody in the bank saw what was happening at once—all but Miss Elsie Cotter. She had come in to make a deposit, and she was standing at Edith Cheek's window. All at once it was quiet, and everybody just froze where they stood except Miss Cotter. She had her back to the door and she didn't know what was happening. She kept right on talking, and it sounded loud as the devil with everybody else standing there frozen in their tracks. I don't know why I remember that, but I can still hear her voice talking away and the rest of the bank quiet as death."

Mr. Walker cleared his throat. "Ted, I don't believe we need to go into all that. Just tell us what happened about the robbery part."

"Yes, sir. Well, there's not much to tell. Out came the guns and they went to work. They lined us up along the left side there, facing the windows, and while one of them pointed his gun at us, the other two pulled all the shades and started taking the money. They had a couple of sacks, just like potato sacks, rolled up in their pockets. When they got all the paper money out of the safe, they told us we'd all have to go in the vault. One of them kept saying, 'Nobody will get hurt. Just do like we say.'"

"Go ahead, Ted."

Ted licked his lips and his eyes widened a little remembering it. "Well," he said, "we started to file into the vault, just like they told us—there wasn't a thing else we could do, of course—

117

and then all at once we heard somebody at the door. It was Mr. Reeves coming back from the drugstore, and I guess he couldn't understand why the bank was closed. You see, it still wasn't quite closing time. Well, everybody just sort of froze again and looked toward the door. I could see his shadow through the blind and I knew it must be Mr. Reeves. 'Sit tight,' this one fellow says to the other two. 'He'll go away.' But of course he didn't. It was Mr. Reeves and he unlocked the door with his key. When they saw the door opening, the one fellow says, 'Shoot him, Preacher.' Just like that. I swear to God it made my flesh crawl the way he said it. Just as calm and pleasant as you'd say 'Pass me the salt.' I remember he called him Preacher. 'Shoot him, Preacher,' he said. And he did. He was a tall man and he had one of these little gadgets deaf people wear in his ear. He shot him, I think it was three times. It was a terrible racket—you know how things echo in a bank—and Miss Cotter and Miss Cheek both begun to scream."

Ted paused and drew a deep breath.

"Well, right about then, before even the last shot was fired, Miz Fairchild jumped at him or tried to shove him or something, and he shot her too. Jake—that's Jake Pratt—he thought she tried to stab him with a pen off the desk there; but I didn't see it that way. I think she was just trying to shove him. Anyway, I guess she was trying to save Reeves, but it was too late for that. It was a pointless thing to do. All it did was get her shot.

"They shoved us all in the vault then, and you know the rest of it."

4

Shelley didn't know how long he worked at the ropes with the knife, but he knew it was too long, and a sick feeling of despair came over him. I'm too late, he thought. By now it's over with and I'm in more trouble than ever. They may come back any minute. They'll blow my brains out when they see this nigger. I'm a fool to ever have tried this in the first place. I should have stayed where I was and maybe I'd have come out of it in one piece. No, you can't do that though; you've got to try. I never could live with myself if something happened at that bank, maybe Helen, and me lying up there afraid to move. No, I did the right thing. I had to at least try. A man has to think of something besides himself once in a while, if he's the man he thinks he is. Now I've killed me a man and if I don't get out of here I'm as good as dead myself, but still it was the only thing to do. Maybe I can still throw a stop in them. If I could just get out to that truck.

He sawed steadily at the ropes, but with his hands behind him and the blade held backward in his hand, it was a slow process. The knife wasn't very sharp. When he tried to exert pressure on the blade with the heel of his hand it slipped off or turned in his grip, and he knew the only hope was to just keep sawing lightly, trying to keep the bite of the blade in the same place. If only I could see what I'm doing, he thought. The rope they had tied him with was heavy cotton cord, the kind used with window weights, and it was brand new and tough. It cut into his wrists like a tourniquet and his hands were numb from the lack of circulation. The tips of his right hand ached and turned weak because of the way he had to hold it bent far around to reach the cord with the knife blade. I'll never make it, he thought. I'll still be sitting right here when they get back. I'm a gone son of a bitch. When they see what I've done to this nigger of theirs, they'll blow me up.

The rain spattered over the tin roof of the barn, and the warm musty smell of manure and hay and harness leather hung heavily on the damp air. A big brown rat darted out of a stall, saw Shelley and darted back again. I used to like a barn, Shelley thought. When we were kids we used to play in the barn and I used to like it fine. I don't like it now, brother. I hope I never see another barn. Look at that nigger, he's not dead. Look at that shoulder though. Christ amighty, I can't look at that shoulder, it must be in a hell of a mess. Look at that hand there how it's beginning to swell. His whole arm must be swelling up like a sausage. Jesus. He looked away and shook his head, still sawing steadily at the rope. The sweat ran down his face and into his eyes and the corners of his mouth. He blew it out of his mouth and tried to blink it out of his eyes. Yeah, up in the barn loft, he thought. I used to like that, didn't I? I used to like it what we did up in the loft. Me and Johnny Stringer and that cousin of his

119

that used to come to visit. What was her name? Mildred somebody, wasn't it? That's a hell of a thing to think of now, but I've got to think of something. Up in the barn loft. I used to like it how she talked. I guess I learned plenty from the little gal all right. That's a hell of a thing to think about at a time like this. I've got to think of something though, I'm shaking like a leaf. I wonder if Helen ever went up in the loft with anybody. I wonder if she got out of that bank, is what I *really* wonder. Chances are, though, that nobody was hurt. Nobody would try to resist them, surely. Wouldn't it be nice if Helen forgot to go to the bank today? She wouldn't though, not Helen. This is one time I wish to God something would slip her mind. Probably she'll enjoy it, once it's all over. She'll get a kick out of telling about it. "I was in the bank when it was robbed." Women are like that. I imagine she got out before it happened though. If they left home when they said they were, they would have been through at the bank by two-thirty. Unless they stopped somewhere first for a coke. Lord, please don't let her be in that bank. Please let everything go smooth and without any trouble, because I'm too late now to help. Too goddam late.

He gave an angry jab with the knife; it turned in his grip and he dropped it. "*Damn* the luck," he said aloud. "Now where did it go?" He groped over the ground behind him, touched the end of it and strained to pick it up. When he did, he felt the rope break. A warm flush of relief went over him. I made it, he thought. By god, she broke! He fumbled nervously at the loose rope, unwinding it and shaking it off over his hands. In another minute his hands were free. He brought them around in front of him and felt a sharp pain run through both shoulders and down the length of his arms. He rubbed his wrists and flexed his fingers and worked his arms and then he cut the rope around his ankles. His hands were trembling. Now, goddam you, he thought. Now I'll fix you bankrobbing bastards.

He ran out of the barn with the knife and down the muddy clay path, not stopping to use the gate but crawling through the barbed wire. He hung his sleeve on the wire and ripped it open to the cuff, but he didn't even look down. He went to work on the truck. Holding the knife like a dagger, he stabbed it into the left front tire. The point went in less than half an inch. Good God, he thought. He made another stab and this time the blade closed on his fingers, cutting one of them slightly across the knuckle. What's the matter with me? he thought. You can't cut a truck tire with a pocketknife. I'm losing my head. I've got to think about what I'm doing. You can't cut a tire with a little knife like that.

Then all at once he stopped and looked up the road. A car was coming. A green Ford. They've already seen me, he thought. He stood paralyzed for a moment watching. The car stopped some fifty yards away and the doors breeched open on both sides at once. The key, he thought. The key is all I need. He snatched open the truck door and pulled the key out of the ignition switch. When he looked up again he saw the tall one standing beside the car with his pistol raised in both hands and held out at arm's length. He was taking a good aim. Shelley ducked and started for the barn just as the first bullet slammed into the fender of the truck. The second shot hit the ground behind him as he ran and kicked up a splatter of red mud. The man tried again as Shelley was going through the fence, but it was a wide miss, and now they were all three running down the road toward him in the rain.

The shotgun was lying under the Negro's left leg, partially covered by loose hay, and Shelley had to roll him over to get at it. He dodged into the door of a stall and got ready. He heard the men come through the fence and heard them running toward the barn, but then there was silence suddenly. Shelley knelt at the door of the stall, his heart pounding, and tried to watch both ends of the barn at once. I've got just about half a chance, he thought. It's a matter of who sees who first, I guess. All right. I'll get one of them. If it's the last act of my life, I'll get at least one of them.

"Hello in there!"

Shelley listened with surprise, not knowing whether to answer or not. They may be trying to locate me by the sound of my voice, he thought. I'll keep my mouth shut and let them guess. I'm in a hell of a mess now. Why didn't I get out of here while the getting was good?

"Slick?"

Shelley smiled angrily. "Slick hell," he whispered. "Slick don't hear you." He looked at the Negro lying at the foot of the ladder with his hands twitching feebly.

There was a long silence and then Shelley thought he heard somebody walking around the south end of the barn. He eased the safety off the gun and got set. Nothing happened. Through the open doors of the barn he could see nothing but a rainy empty stretch of pasture and distant trees. They're wondering what to do, he thought. I've got them bluffed, I do believe. The first one that steps in that door is a dead man, and they know it. I'd hate to kill a man, but I'm the blackest son of a bitch in the world if I won't do it. The first one in. He's it. He's as good as dead when he makes up his mind to try it.

There was another long silence and Shelley's hands sweated against the metal of the gun. After a while he heard the truck door slam shut. They were checking on the gun, he thought. They sent one of them down there to make sure I had it. Now they know they're stymied. Now's when the fun beings.

"Hey, you in there!"

"Come on in!" Shelley called.

Another silence.

"Throw the key out to us and we'll leave you alone!"

I bet, Shelley thought.

"You hear us?"

"Yeah, I hear you."

"We're coming in after it, if you don't throw it out!"

"Come ahead! I got it right here in my hand!"

Silence fell again. The rain rattled on the roof. The Negro moaned and his hands twitched in the hay. I'll shoot you too, Shelley thought, looking at him. I got nothing to gain and everything to lose now, brother. I'll fix that shoulder up for you with some buckshot.

"You want us to take your own car?" one of the men called to him. "We'll leave your car and let you alone if you'll throw out the key to us!"

He's probably telling the truth, Shelley thought. They want out of here bad. But I've come this far, I may as well stick it out. They won't come in this barn. They're not that stupid. I've got them where I want them now and I'd be a woman to give in, just to save my own hide.

Suddenly a shot smashed through the wall of the barn and kicked up a fountain of loose hay. Shelley jumped and his knees went weak.

"Missed me a mile!" he yelled back angrily. Then he thought, you better keep your mouth shut or they *won't* miss next time.

But there was no more shooting, only silence and the rain falling on the tin roof.

"You guys getting wet out there?"

He heard a murmur of voices, then a new voice shouted, "We'll burn you out, if you don't throw us that key!"

I'd like to see you try it, Shelley thought. In this rain you'd have to be inside to set this barn on fire. And the first one inside is a dead man, in this barn.

But then he thought of something that gave him a sinking feeling. What if they brought up gas from the truck and poured it under the walls? They could start it then all right. No, he thought, they haven't got time for that. Time is running out on them now; they're bound to be after them by now. They'll try and make it in my car before they'll waste that much time. I've got them stymied all right. All I have to do is sit tight. I've got the drop on those boys.

Then through the cracks along the left wall, he saw someone moving. He could see a dark flicker along the cracks and that could mean only one thing: someone was walking by out there. He got ready again, and all at once something hit the wall of the barn just inside the rear door. He whirled around and saw a big rock roll out across the hall of the barn; then somebody shot at him from the other side, and when he looked back the tall man was standing there framed in the big open doorway, shooting at him, and the bullets were hitting the planking of the stall above his head with a sound like heavy nails being driven up. He swung the shotgun around and pulled the trigger and pumped out the smoking hull and fired again, feeling the heavy gun kick against his ribs. The second charge hit the man in the knees and knocked his legs out from under him so that he flopped forward on his face. When Shelley shot him the third time he took aim at the crown of his Panama hat and then turned away so he would not have to see what it had done to him.

Now the other two were running, trying to get back to the car. Shelley scooped up a handful of shells from beside the Negro and went through the rear door of the barn on the run, trying to head them off. He loaded the gun as he ran, dropping half the shells in his haste; and then suddenly he stopped. The heavy-set man with the undershot jaw was hung in the fence. He had tried to go through without putting down the sack he carried, and that was a bad mistake. The top wire had dragged his hat off and snagged the shoulder of his coat, and now he was working to get the coat off, straddling the second wire and bent far over, stuck like a pig in a fence. Shelley walked deliberately toward him, gritting his teeth, and at the last minute the man turned his head and raised one hand the way a man might do to ward off a snowball. Shelley shot him again and again until the gun was empty and the shell cases lay all around him on the wet ground.

The other man was gone now, running through the corn field across the road and into the big sycamore swamp that faced the barn.

The fat man hung in the fence, one arm still swinging loosely from the impact of the last shot charge, as Shelley walked past him toward the gate. Shelley dropped the gun and leaned against the fence in the rain. Then after a minute or two he bent forward weakly and vomited over his shoes.

5

The Carringtons and Fairchilds had been taken into the hospital annex where Dr. Clemmons and his wife lived, to wait for news of Emily's condition. They were all there except Mr. Fairchild, who had not yet been reached in Birmingham, and Boyd, who had stayed in the emergency room with Emily. Uncles and aunts and cousins of both families were there, some standing in little groups along the hall, others crowded discreetly into the small living room. Several friends were there too—Mrs. Byjohn and Mr. and Mrs. Clayton, and Emily's friend Madge Whittaker. Madge was the only one to cry. She sat far back in a corner near the canary's cage and sniffled into her handkerchief. Mr. Shallowford, the Baptist minister, was standing with his hands clasped behind him, gazing out the window at the falling rain. From time to time he would rock back and forth on the balls of his feet.

Mrs. Carrington was the predominant figure though, because her anguish was the greatest. She was lying pale and still on the couch, like the principal character at the opening of a play, and Judge Carrington was sitting close beside her with his raincoat still on, holding her hand. They had been like that, without speaking, for nearly half an hour.

At ten minutes till four Dr. Clemmons came walking quietly down the hall. He was wearing neither a coat nor vest, and the collar of his shirt was turned under, as if he had been about to shave. His face glistened with sweat. When he saw how many there were, he stopped and asked one of the men to go in for the Judge.

Judge Carrington came out and looked at him. Dr. Clemmons put his arm around the Judge's back, and together they went slowly away up the hall.

"She's gone, Judge. I'm sorry. There was nothing we could do."

Chapter Nine

At seven o'clock that evening Sugarfoot was out at West End in a cafe called Rebecca's, eating his supper. Saturday was his night off, and he was dressed for it. He had on the two-tones Mr. Kober had given him, a black pin-stripe suit, a pink satin shirt and a yellow tie, and a wide fuzzy gray hat with a red feather sticking up from the band. The two-tones were a trifle small, and he'd had to make a couple of razor slits along the sides where the little toes pressed, but they still looked as good as new. Mr. Kober couldn't wear the shoes because they rubbed his heels; they rubbed Sugar's too, but he could put up with it whereas Mr. Kober couldn't. Sugar had ordered a catfish sandwich and a bowl of chili, and he was talking to Nish and Jim Calloway as he ate. There was only one topic of conversation in West End that night—in all of Morgan, for that matter.

"Well, it was a awful thing," Nish said. "I declare, that poor Miz Fairchild."

"Ain't it the truth?" Sugar said. "And you know one thing? I come right by in front of that bank not five minutes before it all happen. I could just as easy of got in the way and got shot up some myself. If I'd been a minute later, good-by Sugar."

"You lucky," Jim said. "I understand that colored man they had with them got a broken neck out of it."

"That's what they say. I thought a man was good as dead when his neck broke, but I musta been wrong. They look for him to live, according to Mister Neff."

"Broken neck don't always kill you," Nish said. "I had a cousin down around Clanton that fell off a bridge project and broke his neck, and he lived. He went around for the longest in a plaster parish cast though. Couldn't turn his head neither right nor left."

"My, my, they sure picked the wrong man when they picked Mister Shelley, didn't they? All the cars in town and they had to pick him. He don't pay to fool with, Mister Shelley don't. I could of told them that myself. They say he shot one man's whole head off. Decapitated his whole head."

Sugar spooned up a big mouthful of chili and nodded. He was eating with his hat on. "That Mister Shelley a man and a half. Always was."

"I tell you one thing though," Nish said. "I'd about as soon be that one in the fence as that one they after now. They got every police in nawth Alabama after him—state patrol and all. They even got the dogs on him."

"Is that a fact?"

"Indeed it is. Cleve Brown the one told me. He said they went to Wannville late this evening for the dogs."

"Man, I sure would hate to be out there where he is and the dogs on me. That's when I turn myself in, when they call in the dogs. Man ain't got a chance when animals enters in."

"He probably lost to boot," Jim said. "If you don't know that swamp you can get lost in it by the time you turn around. Me and Mister Luke Sawyer went in there one time to cut some locuss posts and got loss big as hell in broad open daylight."

"Lost and it raining and dark coming on and the dogs on you. Mercy." Sugar blew out a long sigh and shook his head. "He neen think he'll get away. Well, he don't deserve no better, of course. He going to get what's coming to him."

"They won't give him no rest tonight."

Just then a plump ginger girl got up from one of the booths and went over to the juke box. She was wearing ankle socks and loafers, and her hair was tied behind in a stiff but fashionable pony tail. Sugar eyed her speculatively.

"You Sugar," Nish giggled. "You too old for something like that."

"Money talks," Sugar said, still looking.

"Yeah, but it don't raise the dead."

They all whooped and laughed and Nish waggled her head. The girl selected a song by Mahalia Jackson and went back to her booth. After a moment the juke sprang to life with a flux of bubbles in pink glass tubes. Mahalia sang, and the rhythm of the music filled the room with a deep reverberant throbbing, like the beating of a huge contented heart.

2

Frank Dupree was having his supper too, downtown at the Blue Moon. He was sitting up near the front of the restaurant so he could watch his cab, and Sybil had taken her customary place behind the counter, picking her teeth with a match. They had covered every aspect of the robbery except one, and now Frank was getting ready to tell that. He had saved it till last because it was the one thing about the whole affair that belonged to him alone, and he wanted to have everything else out of the way before he told it. He wanted to enjoy it.

"Now," he said, "here's the queerest thing a all. Don't nobody know this but me, and I'd just as soon it didn't go no further, if you know what I mean."

Sybil looked at him with interest.

"Pour me another coffee first."

She poured his coffee and waited while he lit a cigarette. He pushed his plate away, glanced over his shoulder and then leaned toward her confidentially.

"It's about Miss Elsie Cotter," he said. "You know her, don't you? Miss Elsie they call her?"

"The old woman with those legs?"

"That's her. Well, I happen to drove her home after the robbery, and she was having the hysterics. She was in the bank,

127

you know. Jake Pratt and another fellow put her in my cab and told me to take her on in. She wasn't hurt, just scared, and she was having the hysterics." He glanced over his shoulder again and then leaned a little farther across the counter. "You know what she told me in the cab? She said she was as guilty as any of them. She said—now get this—she said *she herself* had stole fifty dollars off Miz Morris Walker and carried it to the bank to deposit. That's how come her to be in there." He leaned back to study Sybil's reaction.

"I don't get it."

"Don't get it! Don't you read the paper? Didn't you see it about the money Miz Walker lost?"

"Well, yes. Now you mention it, I believe I did read where she lost some money."

Frank raised his hands and smiled. "There you are. The old girl has done turned pickpocket. Now since this robbery happened, she thinks the Lord or somebody is punishing her for it. She the same as blames herself for everything that happened. I'm not kidding; that woman was fit to be tied, she was so upset."

"Whatever made her tell you, I wonder."

"Hysterics. People always do something like that with hysterics. She had to get it off her chest, see? She had to tell somebody on account of feeling so guilty about it. She even tried to give me the fool money."

"You don't mean it. Didn't you take it?"

"No, I didn't take it. I couldn't afford to."

"I would have."

"No you wouldn't either. You're just saying that."

"Maybe so. I'd of give it a second thought though, I guarantee you that."

Frank stared at her, smiling. It was a good inside story, all right.

"What did she say when you turned it down?"

"Said she was going to burn it."

"Burn fifty dollars? Brother, she *was* upset. I bet she don't though. I'd bet a steak dinner that money never in this world gets burned. That was crazy talk. She's going to think better of that when she gets over being scared."

"That I don't know," Frank said. "But it was quite an

experience for me. You see, they used to be The Family around here. Her grandfather give this town its name. Now she's out stealing. People do change, don't they?"

"You know the saying: shirt sleeve to shirt sleeve in three generations."

"Yeah, but stealing. You can't tell about folks any more. My Lord, this is been a day, ain't it?"

"You can say that again. You want any more coffee?"

"No, I'm going to drive over to the poolroom and see if they's any word about Harry Reeves yet."

3

Harry Reeves was lying as still as he could lie, but the bed seemed to whirl through the room the moment he closed his eyes.

"Why don't you try to go to sleep, dear?" his wife said.

"I can't sleep. I can't even close my eyes it makes me so dizzy."

"Are you going to be sick again?"

"I don't know. I don't see how I could, but you better keep the pan handy."

"It's right here under the bed. You want me to call the nurse?"

"No."

He tried to close his eyes, but the bed seemed to scoot away, spinning into space, and he opened them again quickly. He swallowed and perspiration broke out across his forehead under the bandages. My God, he thought, I never knew what it was to be sick before.

"Does your head hurt, dear?"

"Of course my head hurts."

"You should try to get some sleep."

"I tell you I can't sleep; I can't even shut my eyes."

"All right, but at least lie still and don't try to talk. You've lost a lot of blood and you're weak. Did you know they had to shave your head?"

"Yes, I knew it." He moved his eyes carefully around to where he could see her face, and tried to smile, but the warm tears ran down over his cheeks. She pressed his hand where it lay on top of the sheet.

"They say I'm going to be all right."

"Of course, you are, dear. You're going to be as good as new in no time a-tall."

"My head is killing me. Why don't they give me a dose of something?"

"You want the nurse to give you something?"

"No, let her alone. I'd rather wait on the doctor."

"Do you mind if I smoke a cagarette?"

"No indeed."

"You're sure it won't make you sick?"

"Nothing could make me any sicker than I already am. Go ahead and smoke."

She opened her purse, then hesitated. "Maybe I better not."

"All right. Suit yourself."

Someone passed in the hall, rubber soles squeaking on the polished floor.

"Was that her?" he said.

"Who?"

"Miss Benson?"

"I don't know, dear. I didn't see. You want me to call her?"

"No, I don't want her in here. I don't want her to touch me again."

"For heaven sakes why not? She's the nurse."

"I know she's the nurse, but I still don't want her in here. She isn't clean."

"Oh, Harry, really, I think you must be a little feverish."

"My head hurts, I know that much. It's killing me."

"Let me call her. She can give you a sedative and—"

"No, I told you!"

"All right, but try to go to sleep at least."

"Did you ever see anybody sleep with their eyes open? I tell you I've *got* to keep my *eyes* open."

She patted his hand and gave him a sympathetic look. Mrs. Reeves was a thin, intense woman with a nervous habit of adjusting her glasses. She did it by placing the middle finger of her left hand against the bridge and pushing back delicately. It annoyed Mr. Reeves terribly.

"I think I will have that cigarette after all," she said.

130

"Go right ahead."

"How does your shoulder feel? That's what really ought to be hurting, instead of your head."

"Not bad. Just heavy. It feels like it weighs about a ton."

"They had to put an awful lot of dressing on it, I guess."

"I guess so. I imagine it will give me Hail Columbia tomorrow. Right now it's just numb and heavy-feeling."

Suddenly, without any warning at all, Miss Benson was in the room. Harry clamped his teeth together and stared hard at the ceiling. He was sweating again.

"Well, how's our patient?" Miss Benson said pleasantly. "Still not asleep, I see."

"He won't close his eyes," Mrs. Reeves said. "He claims it makes him dizzy."

"Claims," Mr. Reeves said bitterly.

Miss Benson came over to the bed and took his wrist in her hand. He felt weak and sick with her standing over him. She was too close; he hated for her to touch him. He felt something thick and sick rise in his throat and swallowed it down frantically. After a moment the feeling passed; Miss Benson dropped his hand and went to the foot of the bed to write something on the chart. Harry looked steadily up at the ceiling while the sweat seeped under his bandages and ran coldly down his ribs and under his arms.

He hadn't looked at her at all, but still he could see her. He could hear her, and he could smell the starched, fresh-soap smell of her uniform. As she moved about the room there was a brisk, efficient swishing from her uniform. And then there was something else. Something just barely audible to clever ears. A tiny whispering sound. Her stockings were rubbing together as she walked. My God, Harry thought, it's because she's knock-kneed. He closed his eyes and the bed whirled sickeningly away into darkness.

4

Pete Brayley and Jack Byjohn had stayed with Boyd after Emily's body was moved to the funeral home. They were his closest friends and that unpleasant duty devolved upon them automatically. They made no effort to talk, of course; they were merely there for whatever comfort their presence could give him, and now the three of them were sitting in one of the gloomy airless little waiting rooms of the funeral home, while upstairs (they supposed) Emily's body was being embalmed. It was a terrible thing to think about—what they were doing to her up there—and to avoid it, Jack Byjohn was mentally going over the last round of golf he'd played, stroke by stroke. Pete, unfortunately, had once heard an undertaker discussing the use of a trocar, and in spite of all his efforts he could think of nothing else.

Boyd sat in one of the big imitation-leather chairs with his head back and his eyes closed, as if he was asleep. He was thinking of Emily, and particularly of how she had looked when the last of life was gone out of her and she was lying so pale and so impossibly still on the white table. It fascinated him in some dreadful way. He had known from the first that she was going to die, but he hadn't been prepared for what it did to her. That was the greatest shock of all, the way she looked when it was all over. Not even the fact of death was as bad, he thought, as the look of death.

"Did you see her, Jack?" he asked suddenly.

"No, I didn't, Boyd."

"You, Pete?"

"No, Boyd."

The silence was thick in the room.

"Well, it was terrible, I can tell you that. I can't describe to you how awful she looked."

"Don't talk about it, Boyd, you'll just upset yourself."

"I'm not exactly upset. I'm numb, if you know what I mean. I feel kind of deaf."

"You're suffering from shock. Try not to think about it."

"I can't help but think about it."

They were silent again for a long time.

"Did either of you ever see a dead person?"

They both nodded.

"I don't understand it. What happens to them? I swear to God she looked like wax. Even her hair didn't look real. Even her hair was—"

"Cut it out, Boyd," Jack said. "For Christ sake, why torture yourself?"

"I'm not torturing myself; I wouldn't say this if I were. I just can't get over the way she looked. I've never seen anything or anybody look as absolutely *dead* as she did."

"Cut it out, boy," Pete said gently.

"All right. But it's a strange thing, isn't it? Death is. Take this morning, for example. We were sitting in the living room talking about religion. Only this morning. She was drinking coffee, I remember, and we were carrying on this conversation about religion. She was lying on the couch, just as alive as you please." He looked up suddenly. "You fellows mind if I talk about it?"

Jack sighed and shook his head, and Pete said, "If you must."

"Only this morning, lying there and drinking coffee and talking like nothing in the world was the matter. We had salmon croquettes for lunch. I remember, because they gave me indigestion. She probably still has that in her stom—"

"Boyd, for God sakes!"

"I'm sorry. I'm in a hell of a shape, I guess, and don't know it. You get this way when something like this happens. For a while it gave me indigestion—either that or the salmon. I kept belching while we were in the emergency room. Just shut me up when you get tired of listening."

They were quiet again for a few minutes. Pete lit a cigarette with shaky fingers.

"Yes, it's a very strange thing. Past the wit of man. It's an improbable thing, actually. One minute you're alive and somebody; the next minute you're nothing. A lump of wax. When that happens to you everything you ever thought or did or planned to do is just left hanging in midair—everything is pointless. For instance, Emily had been after me lately to buy a new car. What did she want with a new car? She was practically dead already, and yet she was looking forward to a new car. I don't know. She probably had made up her mind what movies she was going to next week, and whether or not she'd go to Birmingham with Madge. And all the time where she was really going was to the cemetery. I don't know, I swear it's a hell of a thing to try to digest. Now I've got to go home and pack up her things. Her shoes and hats and stockings and things like that. Right now there's a glass in the bathroom with lipstick on it where she drank water this morning. I've got to clean out her pocketbooks, keys and cigarettes and Kleenex. Everybody has to die, I guess. I'll die myself someday. But this is different, when it happens this way. A person ought not to be alive and well in the morning and dead in the afternoon. All those loose ends of life just left hanging. Just whacked off and left hanging—engagements to keep, bills to pay, things that seemed important and didn't make a grain of difference after all."

They were silent for a while, and then he went on again. They let him talk it out.

"It makes you wonder, doesn't it? What's the point of it all? Why do we even bother to make plans and look ahead? I don't know, maybe if we'd had children."

A car passed in the street, tires swishing on the wet pavement. Somewhere a telephone rang.

"I'll tell you something I ought not to," Boyd said. "Emily was afraid she was pregnant. Just today she was worrying about it. And at that time when she was doing all of that worrying, you know how long she had left to live? Less than seven hours. I figured it up. She had less than seven hours on earth. I don't know; I don't understand it at all. You never know when it will happen, or how. Sherwood Anderson swallowed a little piece of a toothpick and it killed him. When I was in the Navy I used to wonder what day, what hour would be my last. But I never heard a shot fired in anger."

"You want a cigarette, Boyd?"

"No thanks. Yes, I believe I will, on second thought. I haven't smoked a cigarette all afternoon. At a time like this you even forget your habits."

Pete gave him a cigarette and leaned forward to light it. "How about food? Have you had anything to eat?"

"No, I don't believe so."

"Like me to run out for something? Coffee and a sandwich maybe?"

"No, I'm not hungry, Pete. Thanks though. I've had this indigestion all afternoon." His eyes filled suddenly with tears, and Pete and Jack looked down at the floor again. There was a long silence.

"Well, what have you heard from Harry Reeves?" Boyd said.

"He's all right. He wasn't as badly shot up as they first thought. He was mostly cut by the glass from the door."

"That's where all the blood came from, I guess."

"Yes, I guess so."

"Emily didn't bleed much at all. She didn't bleed any in front. I guess she had a lot of internal bleeding though."

Pete mashed out his cigarette and looked down at his shoes. He flexed his toes, making the leather squeak a little.

"I was holding her hand when she died," Boyd said. "Did I tell you that? About holding her hand? She wasn't able to talk, but I could tell she wanted me to hold her hand. She must have known she was going." He leaned forward and laced his fingers together. "Like this," he said, "with our fingers interlocked, the way you'd hold a girl's hand at the movies. She died alone though. That's one thing you do all alone, even in a roomful of people. It's too bad, too, to have to die in front of a lot of people. Emily was scared. She was scared to death, and I'm afraid it didn't help much for me to hold her hand. You can't help anybody die. It's tough too, I could tell. She went through a mighty bad time of it."

There was another silence and then they heard a door open and close upstairs. They could not hear the rain, but they knew it was still raining. There was a feeling of rain.

"Boyd, let me bring you some coffee or something," Jack said.

"I don't want any coffee, Jack."

They heard someone walking softly overhead, and then beneath that sound, more felt than heard, a soft rolling of soft wheels. Pete clasped his hands to keep them from shaking.

"She didn't look like she'd ever been alive," Boyd said. "She didn't look like she'd ever spoken a word or moved or ever heard a sound. She was like something—I swear I can't describe it. Even her hair looked dead where it was parted. Nothing could ever lie as still as she was lying. I could have screamed at her or shot off a stick of dynamite in that room and she'd never have known it, you know that? When a person's dead, they're really dead, I can tell you. I never dreamed how still and how much like wax. I've often heard that word used about dead people, that they looked like wax, and they do. They look exactly like wax. But what I hate most is having to pack up her things. You fellows want to leave me for a while? I think I'm going to have a cry."

They got up quickly and went out of the room, scared and sick and full of dread. In the hall Pete lit another cigarette with shaking hands, and Jack said, "Poor bastard."

"How's that?"

"Nothing. I just said poor bastard."

"Poor bastard is right. You know what I'd like to do, Jack? I'd like to go home."

5

It was nine o'clock when Shelley finally came home. Charlie Banks brought him the city car, and Helen was watching from the dining-room windows when he got out and thanked Charlie and walked wearily toward the house. She watched him come up under the trees in the darkness with his head down, walking slowly in the still-falling rain and looking as if he had come back to her from some long imponderable journey.

She opened the door for him and embraced him, and at first neither of them said anything at all. One side of his face was scratched and raw and his clothes were muddy; he looked exhausted.

"Well," she finally managed to say. "You came back to me, didn't you, Shelley?"

"Yeah, looks like I made it after all. It's been a rough afternoon."

They went into the kitchen and he dropped his wet hat in the sink.

"You want something to eat?" she said.

"No, just some coffee. They brought sandwiches over to the sheriff's office to us."

"Is that where you've been so long?"

"Yes."

"That's funny. I called and they said you were on your way home an hour ago."

"Well, I stopped by the hospital to see about the Nigra," he said. "I wanted to find out about him before I came on in."

"He's all right, isn't he?"

"Not exactly what you'd call all right, but he's going to live, if that's what you mean."

"That's what I mean. The coffee's already made; all I have to do is warm it up."

She knew he was watching her as she turned on the stove and set out the two cups and saucers. "Did they catch the other one yet?"

"I don't know. They were still out when I left the city hall. I guess they'll get him though, sooner or later."

"They didn't hurt you, did they, darling?"

"No, I was the one hurt them."

He feels bad about this, she thought. I'll have to watch what I say. He doesn't like this at all. "Everybody in town calls you a hero," she said. "The town's proud of you, Shelley."

"Well, they ought to be. It's not everybody that can shoot a man while he's caught in a fence."

"Shelley."

"It's a fact. I didn't have to shoot that man."

"Yes, you did. They tried to kill you, didn't they? Look what they did to Emily Fairchild. You were perfectly right to do what you did. Most men wouldn't have had the nerve."

He said nothing. His face was expressionless and tired.

"Here's your coffee. You want a cigarette?"

"What all did they tell you?" he said. "Who called, anyway?"

"Mr. Walker. He didn't want me to worry, and he said you'd be on home in a little while. He said you were safe and that you had shot two of the men when they tried to shoot you. He said you did a brave thing."

"You know all about it then. Did he tell you about the car?"

"No, what about it?"

"We brought the Nigra to town in it and he got some blood on the seats. His nose was bleeding. I thought it would be a good idea if the kids didn't see it, so I left it at the garage. They're going to try and clean it up in the morning."

"Good. I'm glad you thought of that."

"How did the kids take it anyway?"

"I don't know. I don't think they really understand what happened."

He was silent for a while, sipping his coffee. "Well, I'm sorry it had to happen. But it did. I just wish to God it could have been somebody else besides me."

"It had to be you, Shelley. You were the only one that could do it. Any other man would have just been scared."

"What makes you think I wasn't scared?"

"All right. But you did it. They picked the wrong one when they picked my man. I'm proud of you, Shelley. I'm *glad*." Her eyes filled with tears and a hot lump rose in her throat.

"What if they had killed me?"

She shook her head and the tears ran down her cheeks. They looked at each other for a moment in silence. He lifted his cup and sipped from it and set it down.

"We have a good thing between us, Helen. We do all right together, don't we?"

"We're the best, Shelley, the absolute best."

"You think I did the right thing?"

"I know you did, darling."

"I had no choice, I guess. I lost my head on that last one though."

"He would have killed you too. They all tried to."

"Yes, I know it. I don't know though." He shook his head. "It was a bad afternoon. I'd give anything if it just hadn't happened."

Helen refilled his cup, but he hadn't drunk much of it.

"I guess the kids are all asleep," he said.

"Yes, long ago."

"They're all right?"

"Yes, Shelley." She felt the tears come up again, brimming her eyes.

"That was a fool question. I'm so tired I don't half know what I'm saying."

"You ought to take a bath and go to bed. Take a hot bath so you won't catch cold."

"I will. A hot bath might loosen me up some. I tell you it was a mighty bad afternoon, Helen. It was a messy business."

She looked away and bit her lip, but the tears ran down her cheeks. She tried to drink her coffee.

"Don't cry, baby."

"I can't help it, Shelley."

"What for? It's all over now."

"I'm a fine wife, aren't I?"

"You're a good wife. The best. You just said so yourself."

"No, I said *we* were the best, Shelley."

"All right. So what are you crying for?"

She shook her head. "I don't know, it's just—well, I know how you feel and all, and there's nothing I can do, no way to help you."

"Sure you can help me. You already did."

"How?"

"Well, you made me some coffee and had it ready. All you had to do was warm it up. You put my kids to bed and had the porch light on for me. You waited for me and watched for me, didn't you?"

She looked at him and smiled with her eyes full of tears.

"You understand me, Helen?"

"Yes, Shelley."

"That's better. We're all right. Tomorrow if the sun comes out we may take the kids and all go fishing."

"That would be nice. Just you and me and the kids." She dried her eyes and tried to get the catch out of her throat.

"See? That's a lot better."

He got up and walked out of the kitchen to the bathroom and looked at himself in the mirror. He looked at himself for a long time, and touched the scratched side of his face and his ear.

"You ought to take a hot bath," she said. "Why don't you do that, and then we'll go to bed, Shelley."

"Is Jimmy asleep?"

"Of course he's asleep. You know that."

"I want to go in and see him for a minute," he said. "Then I'll bathe and we'll try to get some sleep."

She watched him go down the dark hall and into the baby's room and lean over the crib. She watched him, wondering what he was thinking, and then she saw him bend down and take the child up tenderly in his arms. He stood for a long time before the window, holding the little boy and rocking him gently, looking out at the night.

Black Lizard Books

A Hell of A Woman by Jim Thompson
The Getaway by Jim Thompson
Pop. 1280 by Jim Thompson
The Grifters by Jim Thompson
Nothing More Than Murder by Jim Thompson
Recoil by Jim Thompson
Savage Night by Jim Thompson
Port Tropique by Barry Gifford
The Straight Man by Kent Nelson
Blood on the Dining-Room Floor by Gertrude Stein
Violent Saturday by W.L. Heath
Ill Wind by W.L. Heath

and forthcoming:

A Swell-Looking Babe by Jim Thompson
Wild Town by Jim Thompson
After Dark, My Sweet by Jim Thompson

All Black Lizard titles are available direct from the publisher or at your local bookstore. Watch out for the Black Lizard!